There it was again.

A spark. A moment of anticipation.

If they'd been on a date, Megan would have stood on her tiptoes until he kissed her. She might have even leaned in and kissed him first. But they weren't on a date. They were hiding out in the Texas Hill Country. And while she debated with herself about what to do, he let her go and practically ran the length of the porch.

"I'll grab the food," he shot over his shoulder.

There might be a million and one questions about who was after her and why. But one thing was abundantly clear. Ranger Jack MacKinnon was an honest man and dangerously attractive. She already respected him and trusted his judgment.

Getting involved would be easy. So how distracting would it be trying not to?

RANGER PROTECTOR

USA TODAY Bestselling Author

ANGI MORGAN

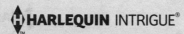

This book is for my agent, Jill Marsal. You're a super person who's always there and understands the neurotic person a writer can be. Thanks for the constant hand-holding and support.

ISBN-13: 978-1-335-63892-2

Ranger Protector

Copyright © 2017 by Angela Platt

Recycling programs for this product may not exist in your area.

This edition published by arrangement with Harlequin Books S.A.

For questions and comments about the quality of this book, please contact us at CustomerService@Harlequin.com.

® and TM are trademarks of Harlequin Enterprises Limited or its corporate affiliates. Trademarks indicated with ® are registered in the United States Patent and Trademark Office, the Canadian Intellectual Property Office and in other countries.

Printed in U.S.A.

USA TODAY bestselling author **Angi Morgan** writes Harlequin Intrigue novels where honor and danger collide with love. Her work is a multiple-contest finalist, an RWA Golden Heart® Award winner and a *Publishers Weekly* bestseller. When not fostering Labradors, she drags her dogs—and husband—around Texas for research road trips so she can write off her camera. See her photos on bit.ly/aPicADay. Somehow, every detour makes it into a book. She loves to hear from fans at angimorgan.com or on Facebook at Angi Morgan Books.

Books by Angi Morgan

Harlequin Intrigue

Texas Brothers of Company B

Ranger Protector

Texas Rangers: Elite Troop

Bulletproof Badge
Shotgun Justice
Gunslinger
Hard Core Law

West Texas Watchmen

The Sheriff
The Cattleman
The Ranger

Texas Family Reckoning

Navy SEAL Surrender
The Renegade Rancher

Hill Country Holdup
.38 Caliber Cover-Up
Dangerous Memories
Protecting Their Child
The Marine's Last Defense

Visit the Author Profile page at Harlequin.com.

CAST OF CHARACTERS

Jack MacKinnon Jr.—A Texas Ranger who protects those around him and follows the rules. His partner breaks enough for the both of them. Recently pulled off of undercover duty because his father was elected senator.

Megan Harper—Investigative analyst with the Texas Department of Insurance (TDI) working for the Texas State Fire Marshal's Office. A very capable Army brat who has lived all over the world and loves adventure.

Wade Hamilton—Lieutenant in the Texas Rangers, Company B. Jack's partner and best friend from college. He has a habit of acting before he thinks things through and always trusts his gut.

Slate Thompson—Lieutenant in the Texas Rangers, Company B, and Jack's coworker.

Heath Murray—Lieutenant in the Texas Rangers, Company B, and Jack's coworker.

Therese Ortis—Who is this mysterious woman associated with an unknown organization? That's the question of the day. Wade owes her a favor.

Harry Knight—Dallas County clerk murdered, but for what reason?

Gillian MacKinnon—Jack's sister. Jack and Gill? Everyone agrees their mother didn't think before naming her after a great-aunt.

Prologue

"Simple answer? It's an out-of-your-ever-lovin'-mind no." Jack MacKinnon spoke calmly into his cell, surprised that he could keep his tone and volume in check with his partner's suggestion. "Did you hear me, Wade?"

"I heard."

"But...?" Good or bad, there was always a but with Wade.

"I haven't asked a favor from you in a long time, Jack. I wouldn't be begging now if it wasn't important. There's barely time."

His partner wasn't attempting to talk him into changing his mind. There were lots of pauses and a tension he hadn't heard since they'd been in the Department of Public Safety patrolling the border. The feel of the call made Jack uneasy.

"Are you in trouble?"

"I've got everything handled—"

"Except the one little favor. I would if I could

get away. You know what week it is. What my father expects. I don't have any extra time to babysit." Whining wasn't his thing.

Or at least it hadn't been. But he recognized the words. Recognized the tired sound of his own voice. Recognized how busy he was dealing with the mundane while his partner got into…what? He didn't know what trouble Wade's intuition was getting him into. Most of the time he didn't even know if it was an approved operation or not.

"I thought I could make her flight and be there when she left the airport, but I was…delayed." Wade's voice shook. It never shook.

"Dammit, was that a gunshot?" Jack asked, but he recognized weapons firing. "Hang up and call for backup. Now."

No response. There was shuffling, heavy breathing like his partner was running. If Wade was in trouble and had still taken time to ask for a favor, then Jack didn't have a choice. He had to say yes. "You owe me, and not just anything. I decide what and when."

"Bergstrom Airport. You should get going. I'll text details as soon as I get…um…free. Gotta run."

The line disconnected.

Wade probably meant that last word literally. But running from whom? Or what group? That was the part that bothered Jack the most. He didn't know which. All he could do was hope his partner was on the right side and not risking both their careers.

He jerked open the drawer with his keys and stared at the ring next to his holstered weapon. Yes? No?

One little favor...

It never hurt to be prepared. He scooped up both.

"You're going to owe me, Wade. And this time, I intend to collect."

Chapter One

Paranoia shimmied up her spine, pinning her to the tight airplane seat. A genuine fear kept Megan Harper where she was while most of the passengers paraded slowly up the aisle.

Carefully gathering her things, she waited. For what? A flight attendant lifted her bag and dropped it next to her. "This yours?" he asked and moved toward the back of the plane, checking seat pockets.

The forty-five-minute flight from Dallas to Austin had been a little bumpy, but not enough to make her feel this way. She'd barely finished three paragraphs of the book she'd spontaneously purchased before they left the gate.

Her breathing was still fast, her pulse still racing. She still felt like something was…well, wrong. She'd felt this shakiness since she was dropped at Love Field.

Thinking back, she realized that was when

the apprehension had begun. Not about flying or plane crashes or anything to make a traveler feel anxiety. This was different. Something she hadn't felt since she was at the San Antonio Police Academy.

That had been ages ago. She'd barely been a cop before transferring to the State Fire Marshal's Office. But still…the sense that she was being watched— Check that. She knew she was being watched. It bothered her that she couldn't pin down the person doing the watching before she'd boarded.

"Miss, is there a problem? Do you need assistance leaving the plane?"

"Oh, no. Sorry."

There was no one left to watch her leave. The unrest should have subsided.

But it didn't.

The anxiety grew with each step up the jet bridge. Alone by necessity for her job, she had no hand to squeeze for comfort. She really hadn't been the comfort-seeking type—even in her childhood.

What was wrong with her? She threw her hand against the wall as a wave of dizziness overtook her. Catching her breath, she straightened her laptop-bag strap and continued. The faster she got to her house, the better.

Strangers were lined up at the gate, ready to fill

the seats for the next flight. None of them watched a crazy woman who expected someone to jump out and…and… Do what?

This is ridiculous. Shake it off. Nothing's wrong.

"Megan Harper?"

She looked up toward the man who'd called her name. When their eyes met, it was clear he'd been waiting for her. He wasn't asking—he already knew who she was. She quickly glanced around, trying to find a free airport employee, but no one would look her way. She changed directions to get closer to the gate, to give herself time to assess the threat. She sprang past the man, toward the security exit.

How he'd gotten to the gate was a question for later. Something about the way he walked, with one hand on his hip, sort of under his jacket, set off alarms. Once again her neck broke out with the pricklies, as her mother called them. She ignored him and had barely gotten three steps ahead when his hand grabbed her arm and swung her back to face him.

"You're prettier than the picture. Here."

Shoving her against the wall out of the flow of traffic turned a few heads for a few seconds. Before she could react, he had her free arm pinned and the other wrapped up in her luggage.

"Back away or you're going to regret this." She

could still use her legs, which were strategically placed to play football with his privates.

With his free hand, he opened a note and held it for her to read: "You have to go with this man to be safe. No questions."

She laughed. "Do you really think I'm just going to walk out of a crowded airport with you? That note is straight from a movie. And I can take care of myself."

"You need to come with me—"

"No way in hell! Security!" She rammed her knee against his groin.

The man doubled over.

Her pricklies were gone. She was breathing calmly when she sort of trotted through the nearest revolving door to baggage claim before anyone could respond to her cry for help. On the other side she realized she'd left her rolling carry-on next to the wall. She headed directly to a counter with two employees for help.

"I wouldn't do that." The deep voice slowed her steps.

A couple of steps away from her, a man lifted his finger in the air. He wasn't the same as the man who'd accosted her at the gate. His serious scrutiny caught her off guard as he guided her out of the way of the revolving door.

"Are you following me?" She looked through

the glass—the man trying to accost her and the carry-on were gone.

"Nope. Someone wants to chat with you." Serious Guy extended a phone, and she heard an unfamiliar voice of a friend she hadn't seen in years.

"Megan. Megan, are you there?" The moment caught her off guard, and she paused. The stranger gently took her elbow, guiding her out of foot traffic, nodding as a couple of people passed and then handing her the phone.

She flipped the cell over and was on a video call. "Therese? I haven't heard from you since I moved to Austin. What in the world is going on?"

"Thank God he found you. Listen, the man with you is Jack MacKinnon. He's a friend and you need to leave with him. Now. I'll explain later. Trust that your life is in danger."

Megan looked straight into aviator shades and an expressionless pair of lips over a dimpled chin. His gesture to wrap up the call infuriated her a little bit more. But when she stumbled it was nice to have him there to steady her.

"I can explain everything in three or four days. Until then, MacKinnon can keep you safe." Therese's voice was shaky with fear. The man looked around without offering any explanation.

"I can take care of myself. But why do you think I need to? And why don't I just go to the police?" She was certain she was capable.

Therese's fear seemed to be seeping through the speaker, affecting her ability to reason. Either that or... Great—the room was spinning. "Why does it feel like I'm on that baggage carousel?"

"Wrap it up. They must have slipped you something." The man gripped her elbow tighter and headed toward the exit.

"Someone's trying to kill you, Megan. We don't know who. At least not yet. And until we get a handle on this, you need to stay someplace safe. We think you're being framed— What?" There was some noise on Therese's end, and the screen went dark, like she'd covered the phone's camera. Then nothing for a long couple of seconds. "I wish I had time to explain and I'm sorry I put you into this position. You can trust MacKinnon. He's practically one of us. Maybe better since he's a Texas—"

The phone went dark again. The connection was gone.

"Can you walk faster? I'm parked in a loading zone." Therese's friend wrapped his arm around her waist.

The mirrored aviator shades he wore blocked wherever he was looking, but it didn't matter. She was quickly losing her footing and the grip on her laptop. "My bagsheze ish..."

Slurred speech and no muscle coordination. Her inability didn't slow her escort down. He lifted her laptop bag onto one shoulder and stretched her arm around his other. She couldn't even protest now. Her eyes were getting heavy, right along with every other part of her body.

"Stay with me, Megan," he whispered close to her ear. "Yeah, we're good. Pregnant. Just need to get her home."

He'd told someone she was pregnant, and she couldn't make her mouth object. Her brain seemed to be working, but nothing else. He lifted her onto the front seat of a giant truck and pulled the seat belt around her.

Eyes closed, her head fell to the window with a thud. They moved forward, and that was it. She'd been kidnapped, abducted. If anyone asked her to identify the man driving, she had a good image of a dimpled chin under shiny, reflective aviator shades.

THEY ARRIVED AT his destination—not hers. According to Mr. MacKinnon, he'd been assured her home was compromised. He pulled into a driveway of a house that looked as if it had been built just after World War II.

How had she gotten here?

Shoot, she didn't really know where *here* was. Someplace she'd never been. Someplace that didn't look anything like an abductor's lair. She thought they'd pulled off the main road at the first sign of a town and then kept turning.

Main road? She'd missed which way they left Austin. She'd been in and out. While she was in, the winding roads she recognized west of Austin kicked in and made her queasy. So she just closed her eyes and concentrated on not throwing up.

Now at a stop, she tried to pull on the door handle. Nothing. Her arms were just too weak. No strength.

The porch light flickered on—one of those energy-saver bulbs that she didn't care for but bought herself. The porch had a swing, a couple of tall-fronded plants in the corner. It looked more like where her parents used to live—more than she wanted to admit.

If she admitted it, she'd feel safe. She'd let her guard down, and she couldn't. She had to escape. Had to somehow get to the police.

"Megan?" He tapped on the truck. "You can get out now. We're here." The truck door opened, and her driver caught her in a bear hug. Not that he was as big as a bear. He just held her tight in his strong arms before lifting her into them and carrying her up the porch steps.

God, her mind was jumping all over the place. She needed a few minutes to take everything in. Should she go inside with a stranger who had practically abducted her? She could trust Therese.

They might not have seen each other in the past couple of years, but when you went through the police academy together…it created a bond that didn't go away.

A dog bayed at the fence next door.

"Hush, Junior, hush."

"Getting out of that truck might be the most stupid thing I've ever done in my life. I have no idea what's going on. Why is it so hard to think straight?"

"Not surprising, since someone drugged you. Not me. I assume it was the guy who followed you off the plane and who has your carry-on." He set her on the couch and switched on the table lamp before securing the front door.

"When would they have drugged me? Why would they? I don't get it. Scratch that. It doesn't make sense. I'm a nobody." Megan struggled to cover her eyes with a hand. She could have been drugged at any time before or during the flight. It was possible no matter how unlikely she thought it might be.

"I have no idea. Your friend didn't bother to give either of us much information." He patted her softly on her back. "You feeling okay? Should I have taken you to the emergency room? To be honest, I wasn't given too much instruction. Other than you needed a protective escort and place to stay this weekend."

"I'm better than when I was at the airport. I... I don't think I need a doctor, but what do I know?" She did feel better than before. "My head is throbbing and every muscle I have is aching."

"I'll get you some water and aspirin."

"If Therese asked you to help me, then I think I deserve some answers." She spoke louder, following his movements through the gaps between her fingers.

He returned with a bottle of water under his biceps, shaking pills from a bottle. Could she trust that it wasn't more of whatever had been slipped to her earlier?

"I think I'll just take the water for now."

He gave it to her and she gulped it down.

He popped the two pills into his mouth and swallowed. She watched his Adam's apple bob under that cute dimple and took an inventory of his brown eyes and the thick eyelashes that men naturally had. Straight eyebrows quirked as he stared back at her, then shook his head.

"No one hired me. I'd answer your questions if I could. But my deal is to keep you safe. I made a promise not to leave you alone. That's all I know until someone lets me in on more."

"I'm not really the helpless type." At the moment, she did appear helpless to herself. She said that she wasn't. Even said it out loud after someone had just drugged her. She didn't know how or where. If this guy hadn't been there, who knew what would have happened? Or where she would have ended up?

"You probably don't think anyone would want to kill you, either." He took a step back and crossed his arms over his chest.

"How do I know that Therese wasn't being forced to tell me to go with you?"

"I guess you don't. Neither do I. But one thing in our favor is that I'm not forcing you to stay. You aren't tied up or anything."

She needed to test that challenge. Could she get up? Get closer to the back door? What would he do?

Even though the house was sparsely decorated, the photographs on the wall really stood out and called to her. She stood and swayed toward one near her—an action picture of a retriever flying into a pond. Water droplets were caught forever hanging in midair.

"That was Birdie. I took that picture when I was in college. She was a great retriever."

"It's exceptional. So alive." Megan looked for signs of a dog. "Is she around?"

"Naw, she died a few years back." He shoved his fingers through his hair before settling his arms in front of his chest again. And he stayed where he was, not making a move to stop her from wandering.

Even if she was stumbling and leaning on the backs of chairs.

"I'm sorry. I shouldn't have brought it up." Her head really wanted to check out that aspirin bottle.

"She was a great dog." He shrugged.

"What did you say your name was?"

"Jack MacKinnon. I'm a Tex—"

"Jack, um…what did you do with my stuff? My laptop? Phone? I don't see my carry-on."

"You left it by the gate. Sorry, but there wasn't time to explain to airport security. Your phone and laptop are still in the truck. Safe for tonight."

"What if someone sees it and breaks in? Isn't that risky?"

"Not too many break-ins around here. Everybody knows me and that I'm home this week. Your stuff is safe."

She shifted to another chair, closer to her goal. "You really don't know what all this is about?" she asked.

He shook his head, and she believed him. It was her job to know when someone was lying or telling the truth. Jack seemed to be completely at ease telling her everything—or as little as—he knew.

"I really need to call Therese and find out what this is all about." She needed to know why she needed protecting. She didn't doubt that she could handle herself when put to the test. But what test?

Oh, yeah, sure.

"I tried your friend. Tried my partner. Voice mail. You're safe and need some rest, so how 'bout we try again in the morning?"

Scolding herself was nothing new. Being in a life-threatening position wasn't, either. Shoot, being alone with arrogant men who thought they knew more than her was something she'd dealt with since joining the police academy. The State Fire Marshal's Office wasn't much better.

The strange new sensation was that she could trust this man. *Weird.* She rarely trusted anyone. Getting her feet to even slide was beginning to be a chore. So maybe she could wait until her legs were more stable and could make it out to his truck. Then she'd find out what was going on for herself.

He pushed his hands through his tangled short mop, smoothing and looping some of it behind his ears. "I wasn't expecting anyone, so I'm not sure what I have in the fridge. You feel like eating? Need another bottle of water?"

"No. Thanks. Look, all I need is a couch for the night and I'll be out of your hair tomorrow."

"Why don't we talk about that in the morning?" He reached forward, and they touched with an electric shock.

Not the kind she'd felt wrapped in his arms. It was a sincere static-electricity pop that had them both waving their hands in pain.

Megan looked between the blinds and saw a couple of porch lights. "Ouch, you pack a wallop." The houses were far apart and she wasn't certain the road—that was at least forty yards away—was even a public street. An older neighborhood in a small town? "Maybe I should call a cab to take me home."

"You could try, but I doubt you'd get one to come here."

"Where did you bring me?"

"We're outside Liberty Hill. It's about forty-five minutes from Austin."

Doubt was back. No matter how much confidence she had in Therese, shouldn't she be more upset about being alone with this guy?

Maybe it was the remnants of the drug still in her system. She couldn't tell or keep her thoughts straight. Why had she allowed herself to be brought here by a stranger in the first place? What had Therese meant? Not having answers was more likely to kill her than a stranger at the airport.

"This is ridiculous."

"What do you mean?" Jack asked, resting one hand in a pocket and the other at the back of his head.

"I need a phone, please." She held out her hand, expecting him to accommodate her. Why wouldn't he? "May I borrow yours or will you get mine from your truck?"

"No. Tomorrow." Jack clapped his hands together and then opened them, palms up. He stood at attention, ready for something. "Our instructions are that they'll contact us tomorrow."

"I am not a helpless victim from a slasher movie. I'm not staying here."

"Come on, Megan. If you need someplace safe to stay, we've done everything right. Why mess it up with a phone call to friends?"

He relaxed, shrugged and took a step away from her. Did he expect her to attack or something? She might have if she hadn't still been sluggish.

"Right." She sank to the couch, finally admitting she was too unstable on her feet. "Don't take this the wrong way, but this situation is absurd and confusing."

"I get it. Your friend Therese was more than a little cryptic." He perched on the armchair. "All I got was that you were in trouble and needed protection."

"I appreciate your willingness to help. Really. But if I am in trouble like Therese thinks, then my best bet is to call the police. I can't put you in danger, too."

She was used to being around officers and macho firefighters. She'd taken a lot of years to study guys, their psychology, their body language. And Jack didn't appear to be surprised by their situation. Or surprised that she was in trouble. If she had to make a guess, he probably had a gun holster under the back of his shirt.

"I'm not worried about it." He lifted his hands in mock surrender. Mock because it was apparent there wasn't a cell in his being that would make him change his mind. "I gave my word, okay? If you can clear things up, fine. But you can't have a phone until the morning."

Even without her knowing him, there was something about the way he held his mouth that convinced her he was serious. Compressed lips with the corner barely raised. Serious or sure of himself?

Jack MacKinnon was as stubborn as she was.

"Why are you doing this? What's in it for you?"

Chapter Two

"What do I get? Not a thing. Call me crazy, but I'm doing a favor. I won't let you down. Do you need a pinkie swear or something?" Jack crooked his little finger in the air like kids did and held it out to her.

"This isn't funny. I have no idea why I'm here or why I listened to instructions over a phone call."

It didn't matter if Megan believed him. He'd keep his word to his partner no matter what. "I'm actually one of the good guys. You'll feel better after a good night's sleep."

Just mentioning sleep had her eyelids drooping a bit. Right up until the phone rang. Megan jumped out of her skin. He'd dropped his phone in the drawer with his badge and gun. She stared as he answered.

"MacKinnon."

Jack hesitated for a moment. Just a moment

while he watched Megan turn white as chalk. Would she faint? Good thing she was already sitting on the couch. Her arms plopped down without much grace.

Jack tapped the speaker button and kept the phone in one hand while he picked up a hunting magazine. He waved it in front of Megan's face while his next-door neighbor chattered in the background.

"I'm… I'm all right. Answer your call," she whispered.

Megan wasn't doing a good job making him think she was fine. Jack had serious doubts she wasn't about to hyperventilate. He was looking around for something he could use like a paper bag to have her breathe into.

"Little Jack, are you there? Is someone there with you? Am I interrupting something?" His neighbor crooned her curiosity.

He was about to hang up when Megan drew a long breath and covered her face with a pillow. Whatever had her freaking out was beyond him. Maybe she was just tired. It must have been a shock to discover someone wanted to kill you. And to be thrown in the care of a complete stranger… There couldn't be much comfort in any part of her situation.

"Little Jack? Little Jack!"

"Right here, Mrs. Dennis."

"What was that ruckus a few minutes ago? Did a group of motorcycles come through town again?"

The pillow landed where Megan threw it, to the right of his desk.

"Nothing to worry about, Mrs. Dennis. I was late getting back. Sorry the truck woke you." Jack gestured for Megan to drink some water.

She shook her head and mouthed the word *no*. She rested her head on the back of the couch. Her eyes glazed over, focusing on a point—if his calculations were right—just next to one of the cracks in his ceiling. Why would him answering the phone send her into a tailspin?

"There should be a noise regulation or something. Maybe you should have your muffler checked out, young man. It's so loud it woke Junior. You know he goes to sleep at eight," Mrs. Dennis complained over her bloodhound's baying.

"All I can do is apologize, Mrs. Dennis. I'll try not to do it again." His eyes wandered to the long, silky-looking thigh showing under Megan's tight skirt. Before she regained her composure, he forced his eyes to look at her feet.

Bare feet. Had he forgotten her shoes in the truck?

"That's good, but it woke me from a perfectly sound sleep. You know we have a busy day tomorrow. You be sure to give Junior an apology."

"Sorry to wake you…and Junior. I understand why you're upset." All he could do was agree and hope she'd hang up. "But while I've got you on the phone, is there a possibility of postponing the homecoming meeting until Monday afternoon?"

"Little Jack, you know a couple of the reunion committee members are driving in from Austin. It would be rude to ask them to drive after work on Monday. So it's better if we keep it for noon tomorrow at Major's Restaurant."

"Yes, ma'am."

He'd always be Little Jack to anyone who knew his father—especially the ones who had worked for his father. And probably to anyone who knew him in high school. Hell, a few junior-high kids had snickered that afternoon and whispered "Sure thing, temporary mayor Little Jack" behind their hands when he told them to stop skateboarding on the sidewalk.

He clicked the phone off and looked at his guest. She visibly gulped in front of him. He waved the phone back and forth, trying to break her trance. "That's the problem with living in a small town. Everybody has my cell number."

"You have a gun. And badge. Are you with the police?"

"No." Hadn't he told her? "I'm a Texas Ranger out of Company B in Garland. Is that a good thing or a problem?"

"Can I see your ID?"

"Sure." He opened the drawer again, thought better about tossing the phone back inside and shoved it in his pocket. He picked his badge up from next to the remote. "Habit after having a dog that loved to chew on electronics instead of toys." He handed her the official picture ID and badge.

Megan took a look and handed it back to him. "Things might have been simpler if you'd shown me that at the beginning."

"Honestly, I saw the guy approach you and couldn't get through security to help. I'd already shown my badge a couple of times. I was more concerned about getting you away from the airport. Then you passed out." He rubbed his chin, conceding she was right. "I don't know your friend Therese. I'm doing a favor for my partner."

Before trying to pick her up, he'd assumed she already knew he'd be there to help. He wouldn't be assuming anything about this so-called favor again. Jack liked a good mystery. He just didn't need one this particular week.

"A man I don't know. Why would Therese tell me to hide from the police, then send me to hide with a Texas Ranger?"

"Maybe to protect you?" Jack mumbled the smart-ass question. He was stunned whenever Megan looked up at him. He'd never seen eyes as green as winter rye. Outlined with smudged mascara, they were still as pretty as they came.

Stop. This woman was in trouble. He wasn't going to admire anything. Not how she looked or how logical she was about staying with him. Letting her stay was a means to an end. He did this favor…his partner would get back in line. Okay, so he could hope.

"It's been a long day. Where can I clean up?"

"Straight through there." He pointed past the bedroom, through the hallway that was mainly hidden from view.

She pushed herself up tiredly from the old couch and looked him almost eye to eye. "For the record… I know how to defend myself. I'll stay until the morning, if it's really not a problem."

Feisty. Determined. Cute. *Stop.*

"I don't mind." It wouldn't have made any difference to his rogue partner if Jack had minded. Wade would have asked for the favor no matter the consequences. It was just the way he was. "You can take the bed and we'll work out what to do in the morning."

She gave him a two-fingered salute and followed the hall. He trailed behind and tried to lean against the wall casually. All of his senses were on alert. The ones concerning his guest shouldn't be, but he couldn't help it.

"Just my luck. There really is only one bed."

Megan turned slowly, grabbing the bathroom doorknob after passing his room. "And oh, gosh. No shower?"

"My grandmother always said a hot soak will do you good. You said you were sore."

Her eye roll said more than words. She didn't appreciate that he knew details from her day. Or was the fact that someone had gotten the jump on her embarrassing? It wasn't important now. He could find out tomorrow.

"Are you going to stand guard? Because it's not necessary. I have nowhere to run…tonight."

The slight hesitation didn't escape him. She wasn't looking to stay around longer than necessary. But that wasn't his deal with his partner. He'd given his word, and the only way his partner was ever going to obey the rules for good was if he kept it.

"No need to waste my time standing here. The window's too small to crawl through and the house is small enough that I hear every floorboard creak from anywhere inside or out. I'll go grab my camping cot. You can take the bed."

She stopped dead in her tracks before crossing into the old bathroom. "Oh, good grief. There's no lock on this door."

"The place was my grandmother's. She didn't need them. I won't barge in. Just hand me your clothes. There's a robe hanging inside that you can use."

She gasped. There weren't too many times in his life that someone looked as shocked as they sounded. Plenty of times they'd acted like it. Especially when pulled over for a moving violation. But this woman…either she had the gesture and sound down perfectly or she'd really gasped at his suggestion.

"That's ridiculous. Ranger or not, I don't know if you're trustworthy. Would you expect your sister to just hand over her clothes to a stranger?"

"I wouldn't expect my sister to be in this position. And I do have a sister who I expect to do whatever's necessary. That is, if she'd been rescued from someone trying to hunt her down and murder her. Yeah, she'd do whatever the man protecting her suggested. Within reason, of course."

"*Murder* is a strong word."

"Unfortunately, it's not mine. Your friend is the one who used it. Don't forget, we're both in the dark here. Especially the part where Wade felt this was the only place for you to stay."

"Who's Wade? And if I knew details, I wouldn't be here. I'd be getting to the bottom of whatever's going on. Life would be a little less complicated if Therese had just explained everything." Megan mumbled the last sentence, mixing it with a yawn.

"Can't you call and ask or something? Surely your phone's okay to use."

Jack couldn't blame Megan. Not really. Right now he didn't know if his partner was safe, either. Whatever had happened, it must be disconcerting to be drugged and told to stay with a stranger with no other place to hide.

"Wade isn't big on phones when he's suggested someone needs to lie low." He really did hope the phone was just off and that his partner was alive. But he couldn't get distracted. This woman knew he was a ranger, but he didn't trust her to stay put. He perched his fists on his hips. That stance always worked to make him look serious. "For the record, Megan, I am willing to barge in or to handcuff you to the bed. Don't doubt me."

"I'm not giving you my clothes."

"Just doing you a favor. Thought you might want clean stuff that fit you tomorrow."

"I have a change of clothes in my roll-on." Realization showed in her expressive eyes as she released a long sigh and dropped her chin to her chest in defeat.

She'd left her bag at the airport. "Yeah. So I've got a washing machine for your clothes and I'll leave a T-shirt for you to sleep in. Take your time in the tub."

He was confident she wouldn't run out the door naked. Or... How the heck did you judge if a person would run around without clothes? So he held off on finding the only set of pajamas he owned. He heard the water and went to the storage closet on the back porch for the cot and to start her laundry—right after he removed his wet uniforms and shoved them in the dryer.

The bathroom window was open a crack, and a "blast it that's hot" floated through along with a "right about one thing" from Megan.

"What's the deal with her, huh, Junior?" he asked the bloodhound on the other side of the chain-link fence.

Jack leaned against the porch post, watching the old hound do his business and creep back through the dog door he'd installed for Mrs. Dennis a couple of years ago. He didn't have an opinion one way or the other about trouble appearing on his doorstep. Life had been simple for the last several years. At least his life.

Now, Wade's, on the other hand, was one complicated mission after another where only he knew the agenda. Why or what his partner was punishing himself for, Jack didn't know. And Wade would never say.

There was one thing for certain. If Jack's partner was going out completely on his own again, there'd be hell to pay. The Rangers didn't operate that way. Sure, they were invited to help with cases all the time, but their superiors decided those cases. The secretiveness about Megan Harper had trouble written all over it.

"What kind of mess have you gotten yourself into, Megan?" she asked herself in the tub. Her voice was nice and alto deep.

Smooth enough that he wouldn't get tired of listening to it. He should probably go back inside instead of hoping she'd spill why someone was trying to kill her.

There was plenty of time to figure things out in the morning with a cup of caffeine so everything made sense.

STAKEOUTS HAD PREPARED Jack for sleeping on any surface for any short amount of time possible. Four years later and the training still kicked in when needed. Late nights on assignment, helping a small-town sheriff or chasing after his partner, who was only an arm's reach from trouble when left on his own.

He'd done his best to convince Megan, but she'd chosen the cot stretched across the bedroom door. He didn't think she'd managed any real sleep at all. She'd tossed all night long. So much, in fact, that Jack had debated waking her up to insist she take the bed. But he doubted she would have slept soundly anywhere.

Megan had cried in her sleep—sort of whimpering, as if she was having a nightmare. Her eyes were still closed when he pulled a T-shirt on, lifted her from the cot and tucked her under his blanket. He'd waited several minutes before sneaking out of the bedroom.

Tonight she'd be in his bed. Period.

"Hell, I'm glad I didn't say that out loud to her." He flipped the switch on the coffee maker and waited within sight of his bedroom door.

There wasn't any way for him to get out of the homecoming meeting. He was the one who needed to confirm the parade route and who would be in charge at the beginning and end. He ended his one-sided debate knowing that Megan would have to go with him.

Clicking on the TV, he texted his sister about borrowing women's clothes and sat in his chair to drink his coffee. Just like he did most mornings. There wasn't much of a routine to follow or disrupt when he was home. Simple life in a simple town. He'd just slurped when the news program splashed a picture of his houseguest in full-screen fifty-seven-inch HD glory.

He spewed. Coffee went everywhere, including up his nose. It wasn't pleasant and the rest was nearly in his lap as he read the accompanying scrolling headline.

"Hell's bells. What is Wade thinking?"

"Is everything all right?" Megan came hurrying into the room, shoving her hair away from her face. "Oh my God. They're using all three of my names as if I'm a serial killer."

Ticking across the bottom of the screen was a limited account of a man being shot in Dallas last night, allegedly by TDI Intelligence Analyst Megan Lilly Harper.

It registered, even if only for a fraction of a second, that the robe she'd slept in was now open. It was hanging loose over the long T-shirt he'd given her and showing the well-toned body he'd done his best to ignore more than once.

They both listened as the news report recounted events from the previous evening in Austin. The little bulletin strip kept running Megan's name and that she was wanted for questioning by state authorities.

"Rethinking that promise not to betray me?" Megan asked.

"Actually…no. I was with you yesterday, so I know you're being framed."

"Where are my clothes? I'll get dressed and we can go clear this up."

"I don't think it's that simple, Megan. They have witnesses, too." *Damn.* "Who the heck do you work for, and what's an intelligence analyst?"

"The Texas Department of Insurance, and I work for the State Fire Marshal's Office. Our agency is a part of TDI. 'Intelligence analyst' sounds a lot more dramatic than it actually is.

I gather information about fires and—" she shrugged "—analyze it."

"The news is making it sound like you're a spy or something."

She shook her head, her long brown hair framing her face, hiding her expression. "Oh, no. Seriously, most of my job is in a cubicle. I have no idea why anyone wants to frame me for murder."

No idea? She was holding back why, and he knew it. "They have eyewitnesses."

"So do I, and mine's a Texas Ranger. I mean, if you need an alibi, I have a great one." She shoved her hair back behind her tanned face, then dropped her palm against the bare skin of her thigh. "Look, I don't know what's up, but you know I didn't do this. Whoever's behind the murder must be using a woman who looks like me."

"That makes sense, but I'm not the one who has to be convinced you're telling the truth."

"So where are my clothes? I need to rent a car and get back to Austin. I made a huge mistake leaving."

"I don't think you did."

Her mouth dropped open. If he looked hard enough, he might just see her tonsils. He was fascinated with how all her emotions were just…visible. No second-guessing what this gal was feeling.

"So we're agreed. I need my clothes." She pulled the robe closed and tied the belt.

"First of all, they aren't dry. I was sipping my coffee before actually doing anything. Second, there was a reason you chose not to stay. Someone drugged you and tried to abduct you. Maybe you should remember that. Third thing—I might agree that it's gonna look like a mistake by not turning yourself in, but that doesn't mean you need to… yet. I gave my word to keep you safe. I'm keeping it. And fourth—"

"There's more?"

"No rental cars or taxis in Liberty Hill. Only way you're getting back to Austin is to hitch a ride. I'm pretty sure that's not the best way for you to travel right now."

"For a small-town man, you certainly take a long time to get to the point."

"Sorry, I'm not trying to be evasive." Nope, he was teasing her and couldn't help it. "I'm a little distracted by the dilemma facing me if anyone finds out I'm harboring a…what? Or is it a who? You aren't really a criminal. Not yet, anyway. So I can't call you a fugitive."

"Please stop. Just stop." She covered her eyes with her fingertips and then rubbed her temples. "I can't think."

"This isn't complicated. Okay, it's a little complicated. Someone convinced my partner to protect you—" His brain screeched to a halt as realization clicked things in place for his guest. Or prisoner. He could see it going either way.

She nodded. "Your partner? I thought Therese said they'd worked with you."

Jack was cussing a bit in his head. Since joining the Rangers, he'd given up smoking and curbed his four-letter vocabulary to consist of *hell*. It was much better for his image.

His partner, on the other hand, didn't have any reason to hold back and wouldn't when he found out Megan was wanted for murder. That was, if he checked in anytime soon. Why would he put them in this situation?

"So what now? How fast should I be ready to go?"

"I'm not sure. This is a bit unusual." Jack hated to think that his partner might be in serious trouble for circumventing an arrest. It didn't make sense. He couldn't get the sound of gunfire out of his head. And he was certain it had been gunfire.

"Well, it certainly is for me. I've never been in trouble before. For crying out loud, I used to be a cop." Her arms bounced up and down against her thighs, the sound muffled by his robe.

"Wade might have a history of jumping in headfirst without checking how deep the water is. But…"

Megan arched her eyebrows, clearly wanting the rest of the explanation.

"I've never known why or how, but he's almost always right." There was no turning back. "The man has a sixth sense about things like this. He said you need protecting, and not twelve hours later you're being framed for murder."

Hell, she was wanted for murder.

"You can't keep me here. You're a Texas Ranger."

"Right." He covered the short space to the door with a couple of strides. He needed to take a minute. Just think of something other than the consequences of going against orders—although he didn't really have any at the moment.

"You aren't seriously thinking about trying to hide me. I don't want to be hidden. No matter what anyone thinks, I'm the best qualified to discover why someone wants to frame me for murder."

He could believe that. If she was an analyst like she claimed, that meant she looked through information and solved problems. She probably had more experience than he did at solving mysteries of this nature.

He hooked his thumbs in his belt and looked out back across the pasture. Mrs. D. waved as she got in her car. "See you in town, Little Jack."

Thoughts were racing through his head faster than he could collect him. If he did this, then *that* would happen. And if he did that, then *this* would happen. He pushed through the emotional tug of wanting to please everyone. A physical impossibility. Someone was going to get hurt.

Or fired. He watched the horses grazing, wishing he'd carried his coffee with him across the room. When all was said and done, he could count on Wade. He already had done so more than once. Bottom line, he should wait before moving forward. Gather more information, but wait.

"We may not know much about what's going on, Megan. But there's one thing you can count on." He paused, waiting on her to look at him so she'd see his sincerity. "You can trust my partner."

Chapter Three

Megan needed a minute of alone time and she was out of here. She could find a pair of jeans and keep them around her waist with a belt. She'd seen Jack's keys in the end-table drawer with his ID and weapon. She would have to borrow his truck and hope it wasn't a stick shift.

There was a second vehicle inside the garage, but it was marked with the city insignia. It would be just her luck if it had City of Liberty Hill emblazoned on the back window.

All she needed was a few minutes alone and she could be heading home. Shoot, she was already wanted for murder. What was a little grand theft auto?

"Shouldn't you shower before you leave?" she asked, hoping that he'd disappear for a few minutes, then remembering he didn't have one.

"I always soak *before* bed. But thanks for the personal-hygiene tip. Good thing it's my day off and I don't have to shave. Follow me." They went into the bedroom, and he crossed to a stack of T-shirts on top of a dresser. "Here's a medium. You're going to need something to wear before we leave for the meeting."

She caught the purple shirt that had a gold panther head on it. "Oh, no. I'm not heading to wherever you're heading. Especially not dressed like a teenager."

He'd slept in his jeans—obviously not his best, but it didn't look like he was changing out of them. Just his white undershirt. She'd seen great ab muscles before, but it didn't hurt to admire some again. Just as long as he didn't see her admiring them.

"Will you feel better if I wear one, too?" he asked, pulling one off the stack and sticking his arms through.

"No, Jack. It doesn't make me feel any better at all." She swiped up the pajama bottoms he'd given her last night that she could pull up to her armpits. She'd chosen to sleep without them.

It wasn't her first time to be half-dressed around a man. She'd been a cop. She knew the locker-room jokes and bro code. She also knew she'd have to get out of here the hard way. She waited until he began pulling his head through the T-shirt and tossed hers at him.

The man had excellent reflexes and caught it.

When his hands were occupied, Megan could have sucker punched him. She probably should have sucker punched him. But she didn't. She ran out of the room, intending to trip him or slam a door in his face.

He was faster than she'd thought. Faster getting untangled and faster out of the room. He lunged for her and pulled her to her knees before she could reach the front door. He covered her with his long body before she could get her arms out from under her when they'd broken her fall.

She shoved. He rolled to his back, keeping her on top of him.

Awkward. But she didn't stop to dwell on it.

"Let me go or…"

"Settle down, Megan. I am not going to hit a girl."

Famous last words as she pulled her elbow free and jammed it into his solar plexus. She rolled and sent her fist into the same soft spot. Now Jack couldn't catch his breath.

"Good thing I don't mind hitting boys."

He coughed and she yanked the drawer open, grabbing his keys. She ran outside and jumped inside the unlocked vehicle. Great—the truck was stick.

It didn't matter now. She'd chosen this path and would have to follow through. Car in Reverse. Jack running down the porch steps. Foot on gas pedal…

Foot stomping on brake when a car pulled into the driveway behind her. She barely avoided a collision but couldn't avoid the half-dressed man aiming a Smith & Wesson directly at her.

"What in the world is going on here? Someone trying to steal your truck?"

"Get the hell out," Jack ordered her.

She put the car in Park and killed the engine as the vehicle behind her did the same. Megan couldn't catch a break, although she might not have gotten too far in a stolen truck of a Texas Ranger anyway. A young woman unfolded her tall frame from the bright red Miata now blocking Megan's exit. Jack ignored the newcomer and came straight to her.

Reaching through the car's window, he removed his keys before swinging open the door and tugging Megan from the driver's seat. "I'd charge you with assaulting an officer of the law, but it pales in comparison to felony murder."

He quickly ushered her inside the house and led her to the couch. Megan couldn't decide if he was more upset that she'd taken him down or that she'd almost gotten away in his truck.

Footsteps on the front porch reminded her that someone else had witnessed her failed escape attempt. Was it another cop or a potential ally? Who was she fooling? If they knew Jack, they'd obviously be on his side.

The witness walked into the house without knocking. Probably not on Megan's side.

"You didn't mention why you wanted clothes, and now I'm not certain I want to know." Her eyes shifted from him to Megan.

"Shut the door." He waited until the woman complied, and then he swiftly snapped one handcuff against Megan's wrist. She watched him scanning the room for something, probably some permanent fixture to affix the other bracelet to. He shook his head and snapped it to his wrist as the anger rolled off him in waves.

"Jack?" the woman said, asking a million questions with his name.

"Gillie, I need a babysitter for my...my guest."

"No one has to watch me," Megan interjected. "You could let me go. I can take care of myself."

A horrified expression crossed Gillie's face. "Are you serious? You're holding a woman here against her will?"

"No, wait a second. I'm doing this for Wade."

"Are you joking? Why would you kidnap a woman for your partner?"

Whoever Gillie was, he didn't answer her. She approached the couch and dropped a plastic sack.

"My partner—" Jack emphasized the words

"—got me out of a complicated situation. He saved lives. Including mine."

"Maybe you should think long and hard about doing what Wade's gut wants instead of him taking care of it."

Megan wanted to interrupt and ask what was going on. They argued like two people who had known each other a long time. Then it dawned on her that Gillie was most likely Jack's sister. The coloring and bone structure—along with her height—were all similar.

"Don't be ridiculous. There are complications that I can't go into."

"Little Jack, I might just handcuff you to the pipes myself."

Somehow the slender brunette standing at the end of the small room looked much more powerful than the Texas Ranger holding his sidearm.

Megan waved her hand, breaking the tension. "If you're serious, I could help you."

They both looked at her.

"Go get dressed, Little Jack. That is, if you have the key handy." Gillie snickered.

Jack silently removed his hand from the cuff and snapped it onto the metal scroll design on the end table. Then he walked away without another word.

Gillie plopped down on the other end of the

couch and turned sideways to face Megan. "Any chance there's a short version of your story?"

Megan shrugged, halfway tempted to remain silent and let the woman continue to assume this was all Jack's fault.

"Lucky for you, I've got nothing but time," she continued.

Megan tugged against the handcuff, but the heavy wooden table didn't budge an inch. "Any chance you could sweet-talk him into giving you the key?"

"Honey, if I had any influence over the MacKinnon men, I would have gone to work for anyone other than my father. Start talking."

"So you *are* his sister. I thought for a second there you might be his girlfriend."

"Oh, please. Jack and Gillie? That's a joke. My real name is Gilleth Anne, after both of my grandmothers. My mom didn't think that through all the way." She laughed. Then giggled. "I'll tell you my exciting tale later. Right now I want to know why you're trying to escape in a bathrobe. One that I gave to Little Jack last Christmas and that he only wears to answer the door. Sometimes."

If the circumstances had been different, Gillie would be a person Megan would want to know. Right now she'd explain that she needed to get home or even call Therese to find out why her friend was afraid of the Austin police.

Megan filled Gillie in on the events. There weren't many, since she really didn't know the details of why Therese had sent him to the airport. But during the retelling, it didn't seem so unreasonable that she would have stayed the night with Jack.

By the time Jack returned, she was finished and finding her confidence again. He stopped at the edge of the hall and stuffed his hand into the pocket of a tight pair of jeans.

He was dressed in scuffed boots, a large belt buckle and a heavily starched yellow shirt with Liberty Hill Boosters embroidered on the pocket. All he needed was a Western hat to complete the perfect cowboy picture.

Gillie whistled through her teeth. "Whew. Aren't you all prettied up, ready for the big homecoming meeting?"

"It was already laid out. I'm not going. Someone is certain to have seen—"

"Seen what?" Gillie asked.

"I thought you two would have a plan hatched for Megan's escape already. Didn't she tell you she's wanted for murder?"

"I might have left a few details out for brevity's sake." She shrugged. Or it might have been an attempt to convince Gillie to become an ally.

"In the name of brevity." Jack laughed.

"Then you, Little Jack, are a kidnapper. Maybe

you should turn Megan over to the appropriate authorities? You don't have any right to keep her here against her will." Gillie pointed to the handcuffs.

"Someone tried to kill her."

"That's still no reason to use force, and you know it."

Jack looked at Megan. Truly looked. As in a deep connection.

Megan hardly knew Jack had unlocked the handcuff until it dangled from the table.

"I can help you." His declaration was uncomplicated by reasoning.

Her belief was unprecedented in her experience. "Where do we start?"

Chapter Four

Somehow he'd made a mistake. Someone had caught wind of his plans. The imbecile on loan to him hadn't retrieved her at the airport gate, only her bag.

Megan Harper hadn't picked up her car at the airport. It was still sitting there. He'd waited. Ready to act. Ready for the next phase of his revenge.

Now she was gone. Disappeared. No one could leave without a trace, though. There was a clue somewhere to her location. He just had to find it.

The hours of preparation wouldn't be wasted. He'd bring her back into the open from wherever she was hiding. Then she'd face the consequences. His consequences.

The printer finished, and he cut the short article down to fit on the board. The authorities would find this and have no doubts about her link to his activities. One piece would remain missing to the ultimate takedown—Megan Harper's obituary.

Miss Rising Star at the TDI would soon flame out at his feet.

SOME RANGER. IT HADN'T taken much for Gillie to convince him to take Megan to her house for her own clothes and personal items before heading on to Austin headquarters. Maybe because he'd already convinced himself when he pulled a gun on her.

Yeah, big mistake.

Guilt, responsibility and honor silently battled for a winner in his thoughts. Guilt had won and was still winning since he'd given in and they were on their way to Austin.

A low hum of road noise and notes from the local country station kept Megan's silence from being deafening. They hadn't spoken since leaving his house. Couldn't she understand that she wasn't a prisoner? She was just under his protection.

Big elephant-in-the-room question was, did she really need to fear the police? His partner said she did. Her friend said she did. The news reports proved that she was in trouble. She still wasn't convinced.

But she was nervous. He observed it in her body language. Her thumbnail rose to the edge of her lips, but before it touched, she would bury it in her fist. Her heel would begin to tap. Stop. She'd put her hands on her knees to keep her legs still.

Yeah, he was a Texas Ranger. He couldn't hold her against her will. Not unless he was ordered to by those getting paid a lot more than him. He had no choice but to hand her over, no matter what Wade's instincts said.

And yet his gut shouted at him that leaving her on her own was the wrong thing to do. Maybe part of Wade was rubbing off on him. It felt like abandonment, and he hadn't done anything except start driving.

He kept his head forward but continued watching Megan in the passenger seat. Besides looking a little tired and pulling at the tight T-shirt he'd given her, she didn't look nervous.

"You're doing the right thing." Her hand started toward his shoulder, but she pulled it back and tapped on the console separating them.

"That remains to be seen." His bad feeling persisted.

"What has you so worried? I told you I won't press charges." Her graceful hand—which had yanked his shirt over her head—made its way back to her wrist and rubbed it for emphasis.

"Honestly, that choice hadn't occurred to me."

Nope, he was more concerned about the promise to his partner. He'd never failed to keep his word to Wade and didn't want to start now. He'd tried calling his partner. First thing back in the truck, Megan began calling Therese. She'd heeded his caution about contacting anyone else.

Neither person answered. They could only leave messages.

The noonday sun bounced off the blacktop road. They were nearly to Austin. He'd have a headache from gritting his teeth if he didn't stop thinking about what he'd tell Wade. Hell, he'd have a headache from worrying what Mrs. Dennis was saying to his dad since Gillie was at the homecoming meeting instead of him.

Damn. More guilt from not filling in as mayor for the week. His sister should be the child groomed to take their father's place. But that was in the future. Now he should focus on the problem in the passenger seat.

"You sure this is the best thing for you? We don't know the time of death for the man you're accused of killing. I might not be an alibi as much as assuring those involved what time you arrived in Austin."

"I'm innocent."

"I never thought otherwise."

"Why is that, Jack? You don't know me. You have every reason to turn me in to the police and let me sort this mess out on my own." She shook her head, and her hair fell forward, blocking his glimpses of her face. "It has to be something more than just a promise. Keeping me in your home could ruin your career. I can't let that happen."

He had to think about that and took an opportunity to pass a horse trailer. Was helping her more than a promise? He'd never worked totally on instinct before. Although his gut reactions had paid off once or twice while he was on border patrol.

It sounded corny, but he didn't want to drop Megan off and step away from the trouble. This excitement reminded him of the undercover work he'd been doing for the past couple of years.

"Liberty Hill only has about sixteen hundred citizens." He tapped the steering wheel with his thumb, attempting to sound casual. "Most kids graduate and only come back for stuff like homecoming and holidays."

She sighed and pushed her hair behind her ears. "I suppose that's true everywhere nowadays."

"Probably. My life adventure was the college my dad paid for, then accepting a position with the Texas Department of Public Safety. I didn't come back home like my dad thought. No one imagined I would stay with DPS and not live in Liberty Hill."

"No one except you? But you seem to have a house there."

"Investment that keeps me from sleeping in a bed too short for these big feet."

She flipped her hair behind her shoulder as she

looked at the window. "You are definitely long-winded for a guy. What does your story have to do with now?"

For all the calm she'd shown in his living room, she was tapping her foot, raking her fingers through her long hair and settling it again around one shoulder. Then she drew a deep breath and started it all again.

"Where are you from, Megan?"

"What?" She turned to him, her nose crinkled all cute-like.

"Where are you from? Simple question."

"I've lived all over the world. My dad was career Air Force. He and my mom retired in the UK."

"That explains a little." He used a red light to check the directions to her home. They were getting close.

"I'm a little confused. What does living on one military base after another have to do with anything? I asked why you were helping me." She repeated all the signs that she was frustrated, then ended with her elbow propped against the window.

Somehow he was no longer confused or frustrated with making a decision. Trying to explain it made him realize he wasn't leaving her alone. She wouldn't be the reason he broke his word.

"I guess things are different in a small town. A

man's only as good as his name, and that's only good if he keeps his word. So that promise you're dismissing is the only reason I need."

"I see. So you aren't taking me to my office and/or to turn myself in?"

"I'll do whatever you need. But until I hear from my partner, I'm sticking close. No reason I can't park my butt in a chair outside whatever cell they put you in."

"You really think they'll— Of course they will. It's a good thing we're stopping by the house. I have a backup drive in my safe."

"Wait. What backup drive?" He switched on his blinker and caught a flashing light in his rearview mirror. "Somebody's in a hurry."

He slowed at the side of the road, letting two emergency vehicles pass. Then turned up the chatter on his radio.

"Did they say Whitebrush Loop?"

It was her street. He had a bad feeling about what they'd find when they tried to turn the last corner. A barricade stopped them two blocks away.

"Jack." She grabbed his arm with that hand he'd been admiring. "They're in front of my house. How can we find out what's going on?"

He unsnapped his seat belt and faced her. "You have to trust me and stay here. Doors locked. If anyone looks cross-eyed at you, start honking. Got it?"

She shook her head. "All these cops to bring me in? It doesn't make sense."

He stepped from the truck and pulled his credentials, displaying them on his belt. Then he remembered the keys and locked the doors. It wouldn't keep her inside, but it would keep a threat out.

The first Austin police officer let him through without any questions. The ones who were a little closer started to speak, but he cut them off. "Who's in charge?" Two pointed him in the right direction.

A man in a suit was talking to someone gearing up with bomb gear. Jack hung back, trying to eavesdrop without looking like he was eavesdropping.

"You think it's a legitimate call," said the officer in charge.

"You've evacuated the homes. Now you need to get the rest of these people farther back." The bomb-squad guy fastened another piece of gear in place.

"We're working on it. I just wish we could confirm she's inside like the threat says." Suit turned to the house.

Jack followed in the same direction. His view was blocked until he took a couple of steps to the right and saw the barricades around the address Megan had given him. That bad feeling shouted at him to get the hell off the street. He casually took a couple of steps backward, then flipped around, hurriedly retracing his steps.

"Get these people back," he ordered.

Megan had said she worked in the State Fire Marshal's Office. Bombs equaled fires in his book. Whoever was setting her up was going to follow through on his threat.

"Why are they evacuating the block?" Megan asked.

She was leaning on the last barricade. Any person with a cell out recording this event—and there were several—could recognize her and wave at the cop five feet away.

Wait. Proof. They needed proof she wasn't in the house and hadn't left his side.

Jack looked like a gawker as he pressed Record and pointed his cell at the entire scene, ending on Megan's face. She didn't question him. Maybe she put the reason together, because she struck a pose pointing to the time on her watch.

"Whatever's going on down there, I had nothing to do with it."

Finished, he laced his fingers with hers and got them back in the truck, pushing her through the driver's-side door. They were half a block away when the explosion shook the ground.

"Oh, dear Lord," she whispered, covering her face with her hands.

Jack had time to look over his shoulder as he paused for the onlookers to run through the street. They inched their way forward while more emergency vehicles responded. He could see the smoke billowing behind them, hear the chaos on the radio—which he turned off.

"Why?"

"The police think you were inside. It's probably the woman—"

"My look-alike they used at the county clerk's murder scene," she finished.

"That's my guess."

"I hope no one was hurt or loses their homes because of me." She used the edge of her T-shirt to dry the corners of her eyes. "None of this makes sense."

"We're almost out of here. Just a sec." Safely on the opposite side of Farm Road 620, he pulled into a subdivision and parked on an unfinished road. "You should probably tell me what's going on now."

"But I swear I don't know." She got out of the truck. She wasn't likely to run away again, but he shut the engine off and followed her.

He dropped the tailgate and offered to help her up. She popped her slim, tall frame onto the gate without any assistance. "When we first arrived you mentioned a backup drive in your safe. Why was it important enough that someone wanted to blow it up?"

"I have no idea. I didn't know the man killed in Dallas and don't know why someone's doing this. My trip was practically uneventful. I haven't connected any dots. There's nothing to back me up. Especially now that my house is gone."

"What's your theory? You have a better reason they blew up your house?"

"I don't have one."

Oh, yeah, she did. Should he tell her that her voice got softer when she stretched the truth? He'd keep the information to himself for the time being. "That's everything I own, you know. My first home where I could choose the colors and plants and even the refrigerator." She repositioned her long hair and shivered. "I'm still paying on the refrigerator."

The sun was warm, but the breeze made it cool enough for a jacket. He took her hand and pulled her a little closer until he could wrap his arm around her shoulders. She could possibly be in shock or still suffering from the drugs at the airport.

He didn't think too hard on whether it was appropriate or not. Especially when she leaned her face into the crook of his arm, not really crying, but her entire body jerked with a couple of sniffs.

Definitely safer inside the truck, but he guessed she needed to be where she was. She took the comfort he offered. He kept silent, waiting for the rest of the story. Hiding as much of her as he could from the road that was getting busier with onlookers.

"I told you the truth." She sniffed. "Most of my work is inside a cubicle. But occasionally I take investigative trips."

"So you found something and took one to Dallas. Why?"

"Actually, I was ordered to go. Which in itself is strange. They informed me after they'd already booked my ticket. I needed to meet with an insurance-company representative who had questions about several properties."

"An owner was getting too greedy?"

Megan sat up straight, turning slightly so she could face him, brushing the makings of a tear away from the corner of her eye. "No, but they all have the same seller. All sold in the past seven months to different buyers. Approximately six weeks later, there was a fire ruled to be an accident. The buyers lost everything."

"That sounds sort of suspicious." He kept an eye open for cars headed their direction, but most were moving away from the streets close to Megan's home. Two additional fire trucks joined the other first responders. "What did you find?"

"Well, that's just it. The sales are legitimate. The fires were ruled accidental. Other than Harry Knight, the Dallas County Clerk, actually having signed as the notary, they didn't have anything else in common." A strand of hair blew across her lips, and she wrapped it around her ear.

"That's the man who was murdered? Is it strange for a county clerk to be a notary?"

"He might be, sure. But that meant he was present at all the sales. *That's* the strange part. Why would he be?"

"Did you mention that to anyone else?"

She shook her head, long curls hiding her face as she looked at her feet. "Just him. I asked if he thought there was anything strange about the transactions."

"You ask and he ends up dead. That's where we start, with that connection."

"Come on. He wouldn't kill himself and frame me for the murder. This situation has to be connected to a different case. I mean, they had someone who looked like me. Wouldn't that take time, preparation?"

"Just a tall, fairly good-looking woman and a wig."

"You think it's that easy to imitate me?" She gave herself the once-over, sort of waiting for him to do the same.

He accommodated her, appreciating every

molecule. But in the end, he knew he was right. "They don't need anything elaborate. If there's one thing I know, eyewitness accounts are never completely accurate. All these guys had to do was get a woman who looked similar."

"And they've already gotten rid of her...along with my house." She covered her face. "That's awful. I'm thinking about my house, and two people are dead. That poor woman. And whatever Harry Knight was involved with...he didn't deserve to die."

"It's okay to be human, Megan, and think about yourself in all this mess. If you don't, we won't determine how to get you out of it."

She scooted off the tailgate and rubbed her arms. There was an easier way to get her warm. He'd never been one of those guys who thought about sex every six minutes.

With Megan...he might slide into the norm.

"Looks like this is what I'll be wearing in lockup." She slid the backs of her fingers down her sides. "We should probably get going."

Jack slammed the tailgate, then checked his watch. He'd only lasted three.

Chapter Five

"That's the sixth time you've called your partner. Is he always this elusive?" Megan didn't think her voice was shaking, but the nervous flutter in her throat verified how uncertain she was about what to do. She had to move forward. Waiting did no one any good.

The possibilities in her mind wouldn't stop whirring around like unpredictable fire. One thought led to another, then another. But sooner than later she landed on the *poor, poor, pitiful me* side of things and had to shake the thoughts away.

"He's probably busy."

"What?"

Jack set his cell on the dash. "You asked about my partner."

"Oh, right." *Concentrate on something else.* "Your sister doesn't seem to like him much."

"She thinks he persuaded me to leave Liberty

Hill. And she's stuck working for my dad instead of me."

"Then why not blame you? Seems like there's more to that story."

"Nope. That's about all there is." Jack dipped his chin, cleared his throat nervously and pressed his lips together.

His phone rang and he answered using the hands-free device. "Sorry I didn't call sooner, Mrs. D. But I've had something come up and can't make any of the homecoming meeting."

"Little Jack, there is no excuse for this. Your father assured me that you'd handle the parade next Saturday. It's huge this year, with over twenty floats. You need to be here instead of sending your sister as a surrogate."

"She's perfectly capable. The parade isn't that—"

"If I remember correctly, young man, you were taught not to interrupt. So let me finish."

"Yes, ma'am." Jack tapped the steering wheel with his thumbs.

Megan covered her mouth to hide her chuckle. The older woman had just chastised Jack when she was the one interrupting. He raised his eyebrows and sighed. *The man does have restraint.*

"How long will it take for you to get back? It will throw off my agenda, but we could move the parade to the end of the meeting."

"I really do apologize, but I've been called out

of town. Gillie will be there. She'll pass along anything that I need to do. I should be back in a couple of days."

"Jack MacKinnon Jr., I can't believe you're shirking your volunteer responsibilities." His next-door neighbor kept talking.

Or preaching. Megan tried not to laugh. She pressed her fingers into her lips, practically holding the giggles inside. Surprised that one phone call could clear her mind of the multiple "why me" traps.

"I really am sorry, Mrs. D. I'd be there if my job hadn't needed me. Gotta go." He clicked the cell off. "Small town. You can laugh now."

"Sorry. It's obviously important to her."

"Homecoming in Texas. Damn straight. Former state champs. This year's team heads to playoffs if they win this week. Yeah, it's important to a lot of people. But not as important as keeping you safe."

If she remembered correctly, they weren't too far from the Rangers' headquarters. All he had to do was dump her there and she'd be someone else's problem. But he insisted on staying with her. She should thank Jack for his help and get her mind ready for an interrogation.

But what about? Did she need to find a lawyer before they went inside? Would she be able to sort through this mistake—because it was definitely a mistake—with the Rangers?

"Do you have other cases that might relate to the unusual fires or have someone with a grudge?"

The levity was gone. Serious Texas Ranger was back behind the wheel.

"I have twenty-seven open cases on my desk. Hundreds more that I've filed away. How am I supposed to determine which one is involved with a murder I didn't commit? Especially without access to my files."

He slowed the truck, dropping his arm across the back of the seat and letting his fingers touch her shoulder.

"Megan—"

"Please don't tell me that everything will work out."

"We're being followed."

"What?" She jerked her head around to look out the back window. His fingers blocked her movement, keeping her facing him. "You've got to be kidding. How would they know where we are?"

"No, no, just look at me. It's a black SUV, dark windows. There's an identical one three cars ahead."

"No chance they're law enforcement?" She identified both of the vehicles and decided the answer was a big fat no. "Call it in. You can do that, right?"

Jack's free hand was already headed to his phone. She kept alternating her peripheral vision from the SUV she could see in the side mirror to the one slowing down in front. Slowing down with just one car between them.

"...that's right. I'm bringing in Megan Harper, who voluntarily surrendered. We're being followed, maybe ambushed. Sure, I'll stay on the line."

"The one in front has cracked its windows. Is that bad? Are they trying to shoot us?"

"Hang on."

Jack slowed down for a red light, forcing the SUV in front to go through it. He pulled into the intersection and did a U-turn in front of approaching traffic. Cars slammed on their brakes, tires squealed to a halt, but there were no crashes that Megan could see or hear.

"The front SUV is caught in its lane. They'll have to make a right-hand turn to come back." Megan no longer hid her stares.

"We weren't as lucky with the rear SUV. They turned as soon as I stopped traffic." Jack looked over his left shoulder.

The SUV was alongside his truck. Outlines of two men could be seen in the front seat. The windows in the back were too dark. Then there it was...a gun barrel.

"Gun," she warned Jack as soon as the barrel appeared.

Horns blasted, including Jack's as he darted

back and forth. There were three lanes on Lamar Boulevard and Jack was using them all, trying to break away from the SUV.

"Pick up the phone and turn on the hands-free."

How he could issue instructions completely composed was beyond Megan. She was a wreck, but she did what he said.

"There are an awful lot of people around here. What if they begin shooting?"

"Were we disconnected? Hit Redial."

She did even though he hadn't answered her question, but it was obvious he was aware. He kept looking, searching. He'd jerk the wheel but quickly rethink turning when it might put another car at risk.

"Where's my backup?"

"It's not working. No signal. I'll try mine." She grabbed her computer bag from the back seat, got to her phone and lifted it for him to see. "No service. Nothing."

"They must be jamming us. They're also forcing us away from headquarters and any local police."

"What are we going to do?" She thought about the woman who was supposedly in her house when it blew up. "I… I don't want anyone else to get hurt. But seriously, I don't want to, either."

"Looks like we're on our own. If they're jamming the signal, then they aren't talking to each other. It'll make it harder for them to coordinate, and I might be able to shake them."

He turned, tires squealing, and calmly tipped his dimpled chin toward the cells. "Power down the phones so the GPS stops. Once we lose them, we don't want them to find us again."

"Sure. Sure. I can do that."

Jack sped up and fishtailed around a corner. She swayed back and forth as he drove with a determination she hadn't seen since her last days as a police officer.

That was right—she was a former police officer. Not a victim.

Never a victim.

She turned the GPS off, powered down and then stowed the phones in the compartment between the seats. Then she unlooped the shoulder strap from her body and unplugged his two-way radio. "Do you have any type of locator on the truck? Anything for emergencies?"

"You just took care of it." He smiled and quirked an eyebrow.

"Do you know this area of Austin?" She did. When he shook his head, she took a deep breath to push forward with her idea. "Since they aren't firing on us, I think we could navigate through some smaller neighborhoods. Places around here have detached garages and driveways that wrap behind the house. Some are big with lots of brush."

"Got it. Tell me where."

"I'll watch the SUV. You watch in front of us. When I say go, take a left. Then step on it, take another quick left. Then find a place to kill the engine."

North Lamar wasn't the perfect spot to try to pull away from another vehicle. The street was straight, but their opportunity came when a car directly behind them slowed to turn. The SUV had to slow, too.

"Now."

"This isn't a neighborhood like you suggested. It's better."

Eyes still out the rear window, she noticed they were passing automotive shops full of large vehicles. "If you can get off this street and turn before they see us, they might have to check all these parking lots."

Fortunately, no one jumped out in front of the truck. The block wasn't a short one, but Jack managed to keep at least two of the tires on the pavement as he whipped around the corner. He kept the pace up, blew through the next stop sign and the next. He skidded to a stop, causing Megan to rush forward and catch herself before hitting the dash. He reversed into a yard.

"Get that gate open farther, Megan."

Across the grass, gates open, truck through and gates closed. She didn't know she could move that fast. She jumped back into the truck before looking around. He backed under some trees and cut the engine.

"Good idea. Great, in fact."

"Only if they don't find us."

Jack turned the key and lowered the windows. The neighborhood seemed strangely silent. Then her ears zeroed in on all the noises that were the layers of background in the suburbs. Sounds she rarely noticed when she was in her backyard.

A car horn from several blocks away. Some hip-hop played. She caught mostly the backbeat, so it must be several houses away. No one approached. No one drove by.

She relaxed enough to look at Jack. When had he removed his weapon from its holster? He had it ready, pressed against his denim-covered thigh. The breeze that had cooled her so quickly on the back of the truck drifted through along with the hot perspiration of waiting.

"I think my heart is finally slowing a bit," she whispered, desperately wanting water. "And my throat is as dry as most of my plants. Well, former plants. None of them survived that explosion."

"I have a couple of waters in the back. I hadn't unloaded everything from my drive down. Let's give it a couple more minutes." He moved his Glock to his lap.

The tension was there in his movements, in

the slight crease between his eyes. But not in his voice. He sounded normal. So did that mean he was carefully controlling everything? Or had he been tense the entire time she'd been with him?

THE SECONDS TICKED by as Jack tried to watch the 360 degrees around them. Behind him his line of sight was limited to the rearview and side mirrors. He didn't want to move too much, possibly making Megan nervous.

Three more minutes and they'd been in the lot for fifteen. She'd drawn in her breath as if she were about to speak, but had stopped herself and checked her watch again. She dry coughed nervously.

"Let me get the water."

She nodded. The *ding-ding-ding* of leaving his keys in the ignition sounded loud enough to alert everyone on the block of their presence. He let it ding and holstered his Glock. He opened the customized side compartment that held his cooler and removed a couple of waters.

From ground level, he couldn't see over the fence, but he heard an engine close by. Probably on the corner. He got back inside and repositioned his holster, then started the truck.

"Do you think it's them?"

"Drink up." He handed her the bottle, then cracked the lid on his.

The vehicle had slowed but passed by without stopping. The wooden fence allowed him to see something was there, but not what color. Maybe the men after them… Maybe someone cruising the neighborhood. Those men were armed and sincerely determined. He was risking a lot parked here and wanted to leave as quickly as possible.

Why hadn't the SUV guys shot at them? They'd been close enough a couple of times. So why not? No front license plates. They'd been careful not to get close enough for an ID. Yeah, they could walk up to him and he wouldn't be able to pick them out.

Megan released a long sigh. Her knuckles were no longer white with fright. She had some of her natural color back. More than earlier when they'd been headed to headquarters.

"Are you this calm all the time? Just curious." She paused to take a sip, then a gulp. "I spent two years in the San Antonio PD. I thought I'd love it. Had dreamed about being a cop and putting the bad guys away. It didn't take long for the golden dream to tarnish. You mentioned the border patrol. How long were you a part of that?"

"Can we…um…talk later?"

"Oh, sure. Sorry." She twisted the bottle top back on and dropped the bottle into a cup holder. "I'll get the gate."

Jack caught her hand, and she questioned him with a look.

"Leave it open this time."

She acknowledged with a nod and jumped from the cab. The bright booster shirt was easy to see. So was his. They'd have to get some other clothing soon. His sister's jeans fit Megan pretty good. Snug enough to draw his attention away from the purple T-shirt.

Once the gate was open, she waved him forward and got inside again before he pulled through. The ride through the neighborhood was different this time. Slow and cautious instead of fast and furious.

"You're turning west. Aren't the Rangers south of here?"

"I'm not taking you to division headquarters."

"But—"

"Not yet. Let's find out what the hell's going on. That okay with you?"

"That would be my first choice, yes."

"Where is your friend located? The one who called you and said the police couldn't be trusted?" He kept to the side streets, a mixture of residential and small business. He wanted to get out of the Austin suburbs as soon as he could but slowed and kept searching for dark SUVs.

"Dallas. Is that where your partner is?"

"Supposedly. He didn't go into many details."

Damn his hide. What had Wade gotten them mixed up with?

"Are you thinking about driving there?"

"Right now I'm thinking about lying low until we have contact with either of them. As much as I hate it, I think we should switch vehicles."

"What are our options?"

"Well, I can't leave this custom truck just anywhere. Liberty Hill is my first choice."

"May I ask why?"

"Did you notice the built-in compartments?" The compartments that had been customized and cost a fortune. "One's a gun safe. I travel with them secured. But several are at my family's home safe since I was in Liberty Hill. If we head back there, I can collect them."

"Right now I'd feel better if they were with us."

"Agreed."

The last thing he wanted to do was face his father. There was no time to have the "I'm not following in your footsteps, hope you can get over it" conversation. But it was the one place he knew he could get a vehicle that wouldn't be traced back to him. No more hiding out at his grandmother's old house.

"He's going to be madder than hell."

"Excuse me?"

"My dad." Shoot. He'd finally felt comfortable enough to release his handgun and began thinking about Jack Sr. All the tension slammed his body again.

"Not to state the obvious, but you're a grown man who's sort of acting like you're more scared of your father than those SUV guys with guns. I know you're a part of the elite Rangers. It's admirable that you respect your father's opinion."

"Wait till you meet the senator."

"Senator?"

"Newly elected. He's not sworn in until the beginning of the year, but yeah, he's a state senator. Didn't you vote Tuesday? Don't tell him if you didn't and for certain don't tell him if you voted for the other guy."

He was teasing her. For some reason he couldn't help himself. Maybe it was because everyone in Liberty Hill revered his father.

"My lips are sealed."

Talking about his dad seemed to relax her. He noticed her breathing wasn't as rapid, and her hands weren't fisted around the water bottle or the armrest any longer. She was also going along with a plan that he didn't really have.

"He's not a bad guy, my dad. He was a Liberty Hill cop, then chief, then mayor for the past fifteen years. I guess senator was the next step."

"And after?"

"I think he has his eye on the governor's mansion, but he doesn't talk about that with me. That's my sister's job now."

"I bet that's the other way around. *You* don't want to talk with *him*."

"I'm that easy to read?"

"Not really. But I had a father like that. Classic overachiever who wanted me to follow them to England after college. I didn't. Too wet." She exaggerated a shiver. "Thanks, by the way."

"For?"

"Last night. Today. Now. We both know you don't have to do this." She gathered her brown hair from across her shoulders and pulled it to one side. "If I could get in touch with Therese or someone she works with, get an idea of who's after me…"

Back on the familiar road to Liberty Hill, he tucked his weapon into the side pocket of the door. Setting the cruise control to prevent himself from speeding, he rested his free arm across the back of the seat. He could easily reach out and curl a strand of her hair around his finger. If she'd been his girl, he would have. Shoot, if she was his girl, he'd flip the console up and pull her next to his hip.

She wasn't. She was a… What was a good term? A suspect in protective custody?

"Do you get the feeling you have something these guys want? They blew up your home knowing you weren't there. They called in a bomb threat to make sure you weren't close and no one else was, either."

"But someone was there."

"We don't know for certain. It could be a mannequin."

"But they murdered the county clerk. And last night, whoever drugged me could just as easily have poisoned me to get me out of the way. I agree—we can assume I have something they want."

"Everything points to Dallas and your last case."

"That's logical, too." She tugged on her seat belt and then crossed her hands in her lap. "We'll get to your secured location—it is secured, right?"

"Sure." His family's ranch? Yeah. Secure. He rechecked the mirrors to verify they weren't being followed. No one was on the road headed away from Austin—everybody headed into town on Saturday.

"Great. I'll give you details about my case after we get food and I have a secure IP address. Now that all the excitement has passed, all I can think about is a huge burger with bacon. I'm starving."

A woman who didn't freak out when men were chasing her. She got angry when someone drugged her. Tried to escape from protective custody so she could turn herself in. And she could still think about food.

Dammit!

Jack was falling fast and hard. It was the only thing she seemed clueless about.

Chapter Six

Megan's stomach growled. Again. Louder, practically echoing through the big cab of the truck.

Jack hadn't said a word in at least twenty miles. If she'd known him better, she might accuse him of acting a bit broody. She wrapped her arms around her middle, trying to quiet her demanding stomach. Then she tugged on the too-tight high-school shirt, absurdly self-conscious that every curve she had was outlined and accentuated.

Well, that thought had come out of nowhere. All right, so it wasn't completely out of nowhere, like the town of Liberty Hill or the good-looking Texas Ranger sitting behind the wheel. He'd evoked all sorts of feelings and thoughts since she passed out in his arms the night before.

There was no reason for him to go above and beyond to help her. No reason at all. It had been quite a while since someone had been unquestioningly on her side.

Wait. Just wait a minute. She had nothing to do with Jack's generosity. He'd given his word to someone she didn't know, for reasons she didn't know. He was simply keeping a promise. That was what he'd told her. So she couldn't let herself get all sappy thinking he was a hero rescuing her.

Another growl tore through the truck. This time, there was no doubt that Jack heard. He laughed for a second or two.

"I think we should get you some food. There's a drive-through not too far from here."

"Do you think it's safe?"

"No one's following. We're not on a schedule—no one's expecting us anywhere."

"Sounds like a road trip. All we need is a local diner."

"Leander has a couple of those." He rubbed his chin. Then moved his fingers to the back of his neck, looking like he was deep in thought. "We need to lie low awhile. Why don't we get a real meal?"

Good idea or not, they did have to eat. "I like the way you think, Jack."

Ten minutes later, after parking the truck a block away in an empty bank parking lot, they were seated. It was the back booth closest to an emergency door in the Leander Southern Café. Classic red plastic booths, menus with diner favorites.

"Meat loaf, chicken-fried steak, eggs and

steak, steak fries, mashed potatoes, corn, green beans... Aw, yes, the American cheeseburger. I see a theme."

"I see extra time at the gym," Jack said, continuing to study the two plastic-coated pages. "You still getting that burger with bacon?"

"It depends."

He looked up. The dimple in his chin became more prominent when he looked curiously at her. The unspoken question hung there as he waited on her to finish her thought.

"Can I borrow ten dollars? All I have is plastic."

"Oh, yeah. Of course. My treat."

"Thank goodness, because I'm definitely starved. I haven't eaten since breakfast yesterday."

The waitress moved slowly across the empty restaurant and looked old enough to have been with the original staff when the doors opened in 1953. She set two glasses of ice water on the table and pulled out a pad and pencil.

"Welcome to Leander. You two ready to order?"

"Can I get bacon on a cheeseburger for here, and then a chicken-fried steak, gravy on the side, to go? Please?" she asked the waitress, but her eyes were pinned on Jack. One side of his lip jerked into a grin. Then he smiled completely.

"I'll have the same with tea."

"Sweetened okay?"

"Yes, ma'am—Nelva." Jack's eyes had darted to the name tag on the woman's shoulder.

Nelva smiled herself. "You two haven't eaten in days, or you plan on driving straight through to somewhere. Did you want a piece of apple pie? Baked fresh and out of the oven about twenty minutes ago."

Jack raised his brows and turned his hands toward Megan like the decision was hers. *Well...*

"Two to go, please."

"All right, then." The waitress finished writing on her pad and stuck the pencil over her ear. "I'll get the burgers out to you as soon as they're ready. The chicken-fried will take a little longer but should be ready by the time you're finished up."

"Thanks," Jack said.

"I couldn't make up my mind. I must be smelling that pie, and it's making me even hungrier."

"Who's after you, Megan?"

"Whoa. That's a definite change of subject."

"I can't protect you to the best of my ability if I don't have all the facts."

"You know everything I know. *And* you knew it before me, since you greeted me at the airport. This line of conversation is becoming redundant." She sat back and crossed her arms in front of her. Then, conscious that it made her look closed and defensive—and that he was probably evaluating her like she was him—she deliberately shifted to lean on the wall and put one elbow casually on the table.

"I'm not trying to be antagonistic. If redundancy helps you remember a detail or two, then let's be redundant."

"I'd rather move forward with a plan."

"The only plan I have at the moment—" he leaned forward, halfway across the table "—is to get you someplace safe."

"What do you do for the Rangers, Jack MacKinnon? Are you an investigator?"

"As a matter of fact, yeah."

"You're on vacation. Why did you come home for a week to help your family but stay in a house that you clearly don't live in? I mean, you said you're working out of Garland. Right?"

There was the surprised, waiting-for-her-to-finish look again. The man could talk her ear off getting to the point of his question. Or he could ask one easily enough just by shifting his features. He also had the patience to wait on her to finish a thought or get to her real point.

"I'm hungry, Ranger MacKinnon, not delirious. I know all the same tricks you do about interviewing a suspect." She leaned forward, meeting him in the middle of the table, inches away from that cute dimple that made her smile. "I probably have more training courses under my belt than you.

No matter how much—check that—as much as I should investigate, lying low is our best option."

Another smile that made her wonder if his thoughts had gone to the same place as hers— under their belts. Oh, no. She was smiling and flirting.

"Here you go," Nelva said. "Easy to get it out fast at this time of day."

Jack jerked himself against the back of the vinyl seats to make room for their burgers. Both of them had been looking so closely at each other, neither had seen or heard their waitress walk across the room.

That was a lot of seconds considering how long it took Nelva to get places.

"You guys good?"

"It looks delicious. Thanks." Unable to wait, Megan reached for her burger but grabbed a shoe-string sweet-potato fry instead.

"Aren't you Jack MacKinnon's kid?" Nelva asked, placing her hands on her hips. Jack nodded. "I'm going to have to Tweet this. Can I take a picture? Well, whataya know. A real, live, honest-to-goodness hero right here in the diner."

"I wouldn't say that, ma'am. We're actually keeping a low profile right now—"

"Carl Ray, get out here and take my picture," she yelled over her shoulder. "Of course you're a hero, Little Jack. Your picture was all over the news during the election. And here you are, eating a burger in my restaurant."

"Who's here?" A balding man who looked like the typical short-order cook stepped from behind the counter, wiping his hands on a dish towel. "Well, I'll be a vegetarian tamale."

"So much for a low profile," Megan said under her breath. She took a very large, amazing bite of her cheeseburger. Either it was truly amazing or she was so hungry her taste buds voluntarily stopped working so she'd put anything in her mouth.

"Go ahead, eat up. We wouldn't want it to get cold," Nelva said. "You know, we watched your high-school championship on our TV. Not the one here, but the big one at home."

"Actually, honey, we didn't have that one yet. Little Jack's game was ten years ago. Remember, the kids gave us this one for my sixtieth birthday." The cook swung two chairs around from the table nearest them. "Man, watching that game again. I knew how it was going to end, but still cheered you on during that last drive."

"Hon, I think you've got your televisions mixed up."

Nelva and Carl Ray continued their debate about what year the TV arrived. Megan swallowed, wiggled her fingers to get Jack's attention, then mouthed "eat up" before taking another big bite of her burger.

"I'm honored that you remember Liberty Hill's state game, and I don't mean to interrupt, but we're kind of on a schedule." Jack pulled cash from his wallet. "Will this take care of our bill?"

"Oh, man, sorry 'bout that." Carl Ray stood, scooting his chair back under the table. "We should go box up those chicken-frys."

Nelva took the cash. "I'll be right back with your change."

"No need. Mind if we box up the French fries, too? We should probably head out."

Megan took the last bite of burger and pointed to hers.

"Let me take these in the back and add them to your sack. I'll throw a couple of teas in there, too." Nelva put the cash in her apron and picked up the plates.

"I'm going to wash up. Be right back." Megan slid across the seat. He grabbed her arm as she passed, stopping her next to him. "You don't have to worry, Little Jack. I doubt Leander has cabs, either. You're my only way home."

Jack really didn't miss his nickname. There was nothing *little* about him. He was well over six feet without the boots on his feet. He even preferred Junior over Little Jack.

The swinging door hiding the bathrooms swished back and forth along with a giggle. Megan had gotten a kick out of Nelva and Carl Ray. Or maybe it was calling him "little." Either way, her laughter was welcome.

In fact, the whole diner feel and food had been a welcome break. Carl Ray and Nelva reminded him of his parents. He could hear the TV discussion still continuing in the kitchen when the bell above the door rang.

A woman and man entered. Not much to notice unless you looked at the dark glasses they both took off. Or the solid black outfits. Jack took another sip of his iced tea, disguising his eyes searching the parking lot.

Waiting in a parking lot by an insurance company was a black SUV with a third person standing next to an open door. The woman looked straight at him with no acknowledgment.

"Hey, Nelva." He raised his voice to be heard in the kitchen. "You got a couple of customers out here."

That drew attention to him, with still no recognition. It wasn't paranoia or even good old-fashioned gut instinct that made him believe these people were after Megan. They were looking and surprised she wasn't here.

He dipped his head in a friendly greeting, then headed through the restroom hallway. Luck seemed to be on their side one more time. There was a door that said Employees Only leading to the kitchen. He gently tapped on the ladies'-room door.

No answer.

He turned the knob. No Megan.

"Psst." Carl Ray waved from the third door. "Back here," he whispered. "Your partner filled us in that you're undercover. Nelva and I can stall while you leave out the back."

"I should leave out the front. Tell her to stay hidden on the way to the car." He pointedly didn't say *truck* in case Carl Ray mistakenly mentioned it. "After they leave, call the police and report some weird characters. Try not to mention us."

"You got it," Carl Ray whispered loudly.

Jack didn't wait for confirmation. He went back to the swinging door but before passing through snapped a picture of the guy's face, then kept walking to the front. He had to trust Megan's ability. She might know about these two Men in Black wannabes, but couldn't see the third guy at their vehicle. Good thing about that was he couldn't see her at the back of the building, either.

He dipped his chin at Nelva as he passed. Her eyes darted from side to side while looking at a recent picture of Megan. The SUV woman asked questions while her partner stood like a character on TV. Did agents actually stand with their hands covering their crotch?

Jack was out of the building, sliding his shades on and taking a look up the street. Turning left got him to a tree-covered lot, so he turned right. If he remembered correctly, he'd have to cross the street to the gas station to make it look like he'd walked to the diner for lunch.

He acted like he was busy on his phone, since he had to pass by the third person chasing them. He wanted another picture to send for an ID. That was, eventually…when he had a law-enforcement agency he could send it to.

The man next to the car had a different idea, dipping his head behind the door. Jack put his phone away and quickened his pace. When he got across the street, he snapped a picture of the license plate.

Passing the doors to the convenience-store part of the gas station, he took off running on the far side of the building. He needed to disappear before they realized he was the man driving the truck.

When he hit the next street, he began looking for Megan. There weren't too many places for her to hide, and since he had the keys, she couldn't get in the truck. In the parking lot, he remotely unlocked the doors and she popped up in the truck bed.

Relief washed over him as strong as when he'd

found Wade alive after his radio had gone dead the second year they'd been on border patrol. He was glad he hadn't lost a woman with an APB out on her. That in itself could have been a disaster for his career. But it was more. Not only had he given his word to Wade, he'd promised Megan he'd keep her safe.

He couldn't do that if she was walking the streets of Leander.

She climbed down and bent over the tailgate, retrieving their to-go order. She handed him the sack and leaned over again. He could take looking at the package inside those faded jeans once... but twice?

Damn, he didn't have time to think about it twice.

"What are you waiting for? You going to put that in your built-in cooler?" She jumped from the bumper with two giant cups he assumed were filled with sweet tea. "What's wrong?"

"Nothing. I... I think we need to avoid the main highway back to Liberty Hill."

"My thoughts exactly. But can we talk about it inside the truck?" She climbed into the back seat after handing him his tea.

He unlocked his gun safe and retrieved two handguns. If it came down to a life-and-death situation, he trusted Megan. They thought along the same lines—like law enforcement. He started the engine, and she disappeared behind him.

"Why aren't we moving? Is something wrong?"

"I'm getting the address of a place I know in Wimberley. It belongs to the parents of one of my...my friends. They mainly use it on—"

"Honestly, Jack, I trust that it's a good place to stay a couple of days. If you think we'll be safe there, then great. I don't mean to sound like a nag. I just think we should go."

"Right. Got it. The back roads out of here are going to take us over to Marble Falls. Safer to go that direction than them spotting this truck heading back toward Austin."

He turned west into a residential section of town. Zigzagging through the homes and ignoring the directions telling him to go straight. He also ignored the impulse to stop at the police station and explain their situation.

"Do you think it's safe for me to sit in the seat? I mean, your windows are tinted and I could look for black SUVs."

"I'll tell you when we clear town. It'll be safer then. We'll be less likely to meet them on Nameless Road. Speaking of SUVs, there was only one. Three subjects. Two male, one female. All looked like federal agents do in the movies."

"How in the world did you get out of the diner?" she asked.

"Walked right past them."

"I don't understand. They didn't know who you were? So do they know what vehicle you're driving? Are we being overcautious for nothing?"

"I think they do. But I look a lot different out of uniform."

"I noticed your hair might be a tad long for a ranger."

Although he couldn't see her, he could imagine the grin and hidden laugh.

"I was undercover and on loan for a while to Brownsville PD." A case that ended well because of Wade's instincts. "Like I said, take away the uniform, the short hair and the hat…different man."

Another reason to trust Wade. His partner's gut feeling had saved his life.

Chapter Seven

"Unit two is in Liberty Hill. If MacKinnon returns, we'll extract immediately. No one will know we were there. Unit three is very close to determining the location of Wade Hamilton."

"MacKinnon walked right by you. Right by all of you."

"I'd like to point out, sir, that we were dealing with incomplete information. A partial plate, an insufficient number of vehicles." Was this guy a numb brain? "Once we determined that Hamilton was involved, we knew he'd turn to his partner."

The ex-agent was either full of himself or used to sounding condescending. The agent was both.

"Have you figured out where he'll go if not home?"

He couldn't believe his horrible luck. Instead of being discredited and dying, Megan had been rescued by a Texas Ranger.

It didn't matter who or what he was…he would soon be dead.

No one could save Megan from her fate.

Death by fire. A cleansing. A purification.

He didn't really believe any of that nonsense, but if the person funding his operation believed it, then he could live with it.

Revenge was his motive. Pure. Simple. Loathing.

And maybe a little greed. Everyone knows it's always about the money.

"I want this wrapped up tomorrow with no possibility that the Rangers will become involved. Do you understand?"

"Yes, sir. We're beginning our trace on MacKinnon's phone now."

But it has to be on, you idiot. Do you really think he didn't turn it off? He wanted to shout the words. "Are you aware of the local terrain? The hills don't always get proper cell coverage. Is that going to affect your strategy?"

"Are we limited to our original budget, sir?"

"I'll check into it. Use your resources and find out if there's anywhere he could hide. That should be easy for an ex-CIA operative. Right?"

"We'll get on it right away."

"You better."

Numb brain and his associates might be good muscle, but thinking the problem through was his responsibility. He'd seen an opportunity. He'd found the backer. He'd found the reason the backer would turn over the money. And then he'd made everything happen.

All he had to do was get Megan out of the picture.

No…all he had to do was kill Megan Harper and make her responsible for everything.

"Easy as pie."

Chapter Eight

"Oh my gosh. Do you know how hard it is to make a good pie? And this thing…this pie is marvelous."

Megan closed her lips around the plastic fork, finishing another bite. All Jack wanted at that moment was a taste…

And he wasn't thinking about apple pie.

"Want a bite?"

Yes, dammit. "No, thanks."

Megan laughed under her breath. Was she a mind reader? Was his crotch swelling? Probably. He came to a straight piece of road and shifted in his seat before the next curve. She just laughed more.

"The house is virtually secluded. I think there are only six homes total down here. Difficult to approach. It should be up this road, then the fourth driveway on the left. Why are you in such a good mood?"

"One word. Pie."

"Any pie or one kind in particular? Does frozen work? I'd like to keep one handy and pull it out during our next argument."

"Fresh apple does happen to be one of my faves." She took another bite, licking the fork again. "But frozen lemon or key lime is high on the list."

Tease. She knew what she was doing to him. But why?

"Thanks," she said.

"For what?" Why thank him now? "I argue just as much as you."

"I have to be in this mess. You don't. You Rangers really are quite amazing."

"We have a long-standing tradition to uphold."

"Look, I made it clear in the past two hours that we should head to Dallas. That's no secret." She twisted in her seat a little to face him. "At some point, you're going to admit that I'm pretty good at this myself."

"That's not my argument."

"Oh, yeah. Sure." She pressed her lips—which he much wanted to taste—together with a firm nod. As if she knew his mind better than him. Shoot, they'd only known each other twenty-four hours.

"So," she continued, "you place a lot of emphasis on keeping your word. As a side note, that only works for people who know you keep your word already. But so far, you've given me no reason *not* to trust your word as your bond. Right or wrong, I believe you."

"Good."

"I'm not finished." She stretched across the console, placing her hand on his forearm. "I'm giving you my word that I'll stick with you until Monday morning. After that, I'll reevaluate. That's logical."

"Yeah, it is." Was he surprised? Had he had any problems with Megan? Okay, other than the fight where he couldn't breathe for five minutes?

Who could blame her for trying to steal his truck? He had handcuffed her. After they talked it out… Okay, so discussion wasn't high on his skills set.

"Maybe I should have…discussed coming here. I thought it was the best move to make considering we got really lucky at the diner. If they'd known—"

She waved him off with her hands. "I'm good with the new plan. Seriously. Hey, the world really does look better after pie."

Pie was not the word coming to the forefront of his mind. He parked the truck close to the side of the house, pointed in the direction to leave. When he got out, he pulled as much oxygen into his lungs as possible, then bent over to stretch his back. By the time he stood straight, Megan was in front of him.

"Nice place. Where's the key?"

He led the way to the back porch and pulled down a birdhouse, popping the bottom off and finding the spare key. Good thing it was there, or the past two hours of disagreeing would have been several more of *I told you so*.

"Oh my God, this place is beautiful."

"But? I hear it in your voice."

"You can? The strategic part of me is fearful that we're boxed in with no place to run."

"At the same time, there's only one way in, and we'll see anyone who approaches on the private drive." He unlocked the door to the living area, then crossed the covered dog run and unlocked the bedrooms.

Megan was already inside. "See who's coming is right. There's nothing but windows. Look up there." She pointed. "A bird tried to fly through."

Sure enough, there was an imprint of a bird in flight. The weeds had grown up around the front, and there was a lot of brush between the house and the road. Both would make it harder to see an attack. But the other side of the house…

"This is amazing. How close are we to the river—or is it a creek?" Megan went to the wall of glass doors and immediately unlocked them.

"Lone Man Creek. I'd say about sixty yards."

He joined her walking back onto the porch that ran the length of the house. "The rock face isn't high but makes it hard to approach from that direction. We should walk the riverbed and I'll show you some ways to get out on foot."

"Do you climb?"

"As in rock climbing? Not really."

"So is that a yes or no?"

"No," he admitted. "Not really my thing."

"I've done some traditional climbing, but never free solo. Too freaking dangerous for my taste, or my dad's. We climbed all over the world before his retirement." She bounced off the porch to gain a better look. "You aren't afraid of heights, are you?"

"I wouldn't say afraid. I just have a healthy respect for falling." He joined her.

A sound to their left had them both freezing. He raised his finger to his lips. No one had them in their crosshairs.

"Oh, wow. I don't think I've ever been this close to a deer before. I mean, well, not even in a zoo."

"Let me close the door and we'll take a look at the creek before it's dark. They might even have rubber boots you can wear."

"Good idea."

Megan waited and listened. Nothing. Then what she thought was silence became relaxation at its finest. Sounds of the creek echoed against the limestone bluff and the bend that wasn't far away. Birds settling. Locusts.

It would be easy to let her guard down in a place like this.

The sun was beginning to sink to the edge of the bluff. She searched for a way down the hill. Nothing permanent. No stairs, no clear-cut path, no pushed-aside grass. Just two Adirondack chairs and a stump that could be used as a table.

The deer hadn't been frightened. It stayed close, chomping on the drying grass and drifting farther away. She took a classic, deep relaxing breath. Part of the arguing earlier was a mix of adrenaline and being in the dark.

Her curiosity and need to investigate was why she'd joined the fire marshal's office at TDI as quickly as she had. And yet most of the time she felt like an accountant, studying numbers and assessing response times of fire departments.

She'd grown to appreciate the times she'd been in the field searching for answers about warehouse fires. Following the arson investigators, talking to them about the path and reason the fire had spread, hoping for a reason to do it again. The few home fire questions she'd had she never wanted to repeat. A family losing everything was just horrible.

"Ready?"

She jumped at his baritone voice catching her so deep in thought. "You're prepared."

He held a flashlight and a pair of rubber boots that certainly beat the flip-flops his sister had lent her. "They may be a little big but will protect you from sticker vines and bugs."

Glad her heels were safely tucked inside the back-seat pocket in the truck, she sat on the edge of the porch that was more like an extension of the house. He was right   the boots were too big, but she could certainly explore in them.

"How far from town are we?" she asked as they started down the steep incline.

"It takes about half an hour. Why?"

"I'd like to find a place that's safe to access my files remotely, but I don't want to alert anyone where we are." She grabbed a tree to keep from slipping and quickly yanked it back.

"Here." Jack stepped around her. "Let me go first. Those cypress trees are sturdy but rough on your hands."

"Are your boots slick on this loose rock?"

"Everything's slick when the rocks are rolling under your feet. Don't worry. I got you." He dug his heels into the ground, and she followed his lead.

One almost slip and both her hands were quickly on his shoulders. She lifted one and a second later had both touching him again. He tapped her hands to keep them there.

It took about five harrowing minutes, but they found a way to the rock embankment. With both his feet on rocky ground, he turned to help her with the last one-foot drop. Hands at her waist, her hands on his shoulders, he lifted and they stood there...waiting.

Did he feel the anticipation spark as her lips passed his? It sure felt like he did. His heart was beating just a little faster when her palms slid down his chest. Yeah, she couldn't help herself.

There was an attraction. She could fight it and say they shouldn't move forward because of the obvious reasons. Or she could ignore the professional side of her brain and admit there was a connection. A connection that was getting stronger with each look and definitely each touch.

He dropped his hands like she was on fire, giving her even more of a reason to believe he was thinking the same thoughts.

"West takes us to Red Hawke Road. There are five or six houses that may or may not be occupied. Some are right on the creek. Others aren't."

"And to the east?" She splashed into the cold water and faced that direction.

"I believe that's our best option to lose men chasing us. There aren't too many homes before it turns into the Halifax Ranch. Lots of acreage once we get there. Old Indian caves, bluffs, the Blanco River. There's a small dam and road that might throw them off, too."

"You already made up your mind which way we're going."

"Pretty much."

"Thanks for being considerate about it, though."

Jack made her feel included. She had no idea if this was deliberate in order to confuse her or if he was genuine. *Scratch that.* He was the genuine article. There was no talking herself out of that impression.

Under the bluff, darkness was steadily moving in. She stepped into the middle of the shallow creek, careful not to slip and drench herself, but there was nothing to see. No lights from nearby houses. No light pollution from a nearby town.

They really were in the middle of nowhere.

A good place to analyze and organize.

"You're shivering. Ready to go up? There are some electric blankets or I could start a fire."

"Dinner in front of the fire? Will there be a movie, too?"

"Only if you like a DVD they have. I didn't pay much attention to those when I was here before."

They started back up the incline. Jack led the way, holding her hand, steadying her when the rubber boots slipped. Back to the deck, he stepped up, then lifted her with both hands.

There it was again.

A spark. A moment of anticipation.

If they'd been on a date, she would have stood on her tiptoes until he kissed her. She might have even leaned in and kissed him first. But they weren't on a date. They were hiding out in the Texas Hill Country. And while she debated with herself about what to do, he let her go and practically ran the length of the porch.

"I'll grab the food," he shot over his shoulder.

There might be a million and one questions about who was after her and why. But one thing was abundantly clear. Ranger Jack MacKinnon was an honest man and dangerously attractive. She already respected him and trusted his judgment.

Getting involved would be easy. So how distracting would it be trying not to?

Chapter Nine

Megan was wrapped in a blanket when he returned to the porch. She stood at the thermostat, probably cranking up the heat, the wolf-patterned throw draped around her shoulders.

He had their chicken-fried-steak bag in one hand and some small logs under his arm. He stayed where he was, just watching.

Remembering.

Finding the house after two years had been easier than he thought. He'd turned his phone off a second time after a quick look at the map. He thought he'd need the GPS when he got closer. But even finding the overgrown driveway had been easy.

Stopping the memories…he tried, but it didn't work. Jack could already smell the cedar burning in the fireplace. Toni loved fires. They'd had one every night they'd been here. A romantic dinner in Wimberley and he'd popped the question under the stars with a bottle of wine.

Thank God there had been two bedrooms after she'd said no.

Never ask a question you don't know the answer to. Yeah, that was the advice his dad had given him afterward.

Too bad he couldn't have mentioned that *before* he'd asked. She'd told him she loved him; that wasn't the problem. Being in law enforcement—on the street or behind a desk—it didn't matter. She'd taken off to Europe soon after that, and he hadn't seen her since.

Life moved on, but luckily her parents still kept a spare key in the birdhouse. And double luck that they weren't here for the weekend.

Being at the house was a wake-up call of why he didn't want to get involved. *Dammit!* Why was the thought of getting involved with Megan even entering his mind? Until he heard differently from Wade, he had to go with the state's version of events. That meant he would take her to headquarters on Monday morning.

It didn't matter what Wade wanted any longer. Or Megan.

Austin was about two hours from here. Faster when you needed to put the woman who told you she just wanted to be friends on a plane back to Dallas.

He stomped, knocking the dirt and leaves off his boots, alerting Megan that he was coming inside. He didn't want to startle her—just in case she had a weapon hidden under the wolf.

"You ready for dinner?" he asked, closing the door behind him.

He dropped the wood next to the fireplace and stacked it at the edge of the hearth.

"Jack, can I ask you something?"

"Sure."

"I've been thinking. Why would your partner put you in a position of protecting me? I mean, why bring you in at the last moment without a heads-up?"

"You don't know Wade."

"Is that a question?"

"I was undercover on and off for the last year, working some contacts I had before I joined the Rangers. During that time, my partner discovered he had a knack for finding trouble—as in the law-breaking kind." Jack pulled the to-go order from the bag. He drew out a new trash bag with the intention of throwing it in the back of the truck when they left.

If he was lucky, no one would be able to tell they were there.

"So you are on vacation and he had nothing to do and just happened to discover that someone's trying to kill me?"

"That sounds about right. Of course, it wasn't much of a vacation. I came back for a high-school reunion and to help my dad."

"You really think that your partner just stumbled on information?" She made a sound like he was crazy for believing that.

"I know that Wade has contacts that I know nothing about. I also know that if there's corrupt cops or state officials, we're the guys they call to clean it up."

"We as in the Rangers?"

"I also know that I trust my partner and that he'll call in a couple of days. That's what he said. It's been one. We need to wait until Monday."

"Oh, I am. I told you I would." She curled her legs under her and the wolf on the couch.

Everything was exactly the same as when he'd been here before. The heat had kicked on and the room warmed up—or he was feeling the pressure of illegal entry.

"Still want the fire?"

"Please."

He set the basics and lit the kindling.

TDI Analyst Harper had to know more than she was telling him. Or maybe she didn't know what she knew? That was a real possibility. If the professionals he'd seen that afternoon found them...

What would he do?

The answer stunned him. Was he *that* attracted

to this woman wanted for questioning for a murder? Dammit, he was willing to take those men out. He believed she was innocent and was determined to defend her.

The fire was crackling and popping. Megan moved one of the chairs closer, left the wolf blanket and walked behind him to open cabinets. He'd remembered how to get here and how to get inside, but he didn't know where the plates were. So he let her look.

After finding a plate, she stood in front of the open refrigerator door. "Too bad all the tea's gone."

"I could brew some."

"It's okay. Do you think your friends would mind if I took a beer?"

"I doubt they'll notice it's gone. Or if two are."

She took the hint, grabbed two and twisted the tops off, then handed him one before leaning on the granite island countertop. He heated the food in the microwave and they stood in silence, drinking and waiting.

Was he really that boring? He used to be fun. Hell, she'd accused him that morning of using too many words to get to the point. Now he couldn't think of a thing to say.

Undercover, that hadn't been a problem. He hadn't allowed himself to relax with anyone. Megan was the first woman in two years with whom he could be himself. Maybe it was just being at this house—where he'd failed—that made his brain stop.

Did he remember how to *not* be serious? Maybe it was time to find out. Maybe this woman was the one to find out with? She certainly was nice to look at. He had to force himself to look straight ahead and not tilt his head and get an even better look at her propped up against the counter.

But he didn't have to stare at her to remember how nice her eyes were. Framed all day with the barest of eyeliner and mascara. He'd watched her put it on at his house, mentioning to Gillie that she was thankful to have backups in her laptop bag.

Even with her in his sister's jeans, he couldn't stop admiring one of the nicest behinds he'd watched in a while. He'd gotten an eyeful while she paced the length of his living room that morning convincing him to take her to headquarters.

The rest of her curves were hidden under the wolf blanket again. Not completely hidden. Every now and then he got a peek at her smooth tanned skin. He liked the idea of seeing her on a white-sand beach, turning a shade darker in a bikini.

JACK WAS ACTING a little weird. Well, maybe this was normal. How would she know? It was hard to remember that they'd only met the day before when he'd saved her from being abducted.

The microwave dinged. Food was ready.

"Table or fire?"

"I'm getting as close to that fire as possible. I've always loved the fires my dad and I had camping. We never had a fireplace inside. They still don't in England."

Now maybe she was acting weird. Hyperaware of him. Hyperaware she liked him…a lot. And hyperaware that she was babbling like the village idiot. She focused on her meal.

She finished and poked the fire to make it pop again until she couldn't handle not knowing. "What now?"

"They have a nice selection of DVDs. They're on the shelf in the closet."

"That's not what I mean, and you know it."

His look and sigh of resignation told her he did know exactly what she meant.

He set his empty plate on the coffee table. "Let's take it one step at a time. We might be running for our lives down that creek in the morning."

She couldn't dwell on the fact that she was wanted by the police and ruthless killers who had murdered at least two people that they knew about. Panicking wasn't her style. Granted, she'd never been in a similar situation, but freaking out wouldn't help.

"Without access to my files, I can't begin to narrow down who might actually be involved.

Without contacting Therese or your partner, I'm not sure if we can even formulate a plan."

"Even if we could, it's all contingent on what we're told Monday. I still think our best bet is to sit tight and wait. As long as those black SUVs don't find us."

"You didn't answer me about going into town for internet." She tried to be casual about asking. He might have said they'd wait without a plan, but her brain didn't work that way. She wanted one. Sort of needed one.

Jack was clearly not going to discuss tomorrow. Potential plans aside, she pointedly looked around the large rectangular room.

"Are there bedrooms and a shower on the other half of the house? I found the toilet by the laundry and figured if people stayed here they didn't bathe in the ice water of the creek."

Jack laughed. Finally. It was good to see his dimples back.

"It's good to see you taking this all in stride," he said.

"You seem surprised. To be honest, I'm a little surprised myself about how well I'm holding it together."

"I've been around women who wouldn't have."

"It must be because I'm a military brat. I have a different makeup than most females."

"An admirable one."

Wait a minute. After two hours on a couch in a dark room, watching a cozy movie in a very romantic house at the end of most roads… Who would blame her for melting into his arms?

"You know…we probably don't need the complication of being together more than we're already together. So can you tone down the charm… and the dimples?"

"I have dimples?"

"Cut it out." If she'd been next to him she would have pushed on his shoulder. He would have leaned back a little closer. She could see it all playing out. Getting more comfortable with each other. Flirting a little more with each line.

"To answer your earlier question, there are two bedrooms and a shared bath across the porch. There's also a Murphy bed in the wall by the kitchen. You can take either bedroom you want. I'm not sleeping for a while. I want to make sure no one has followed."

"I can stay up—"

"No." He stood, lifting his plate, then hers. "You're right about complicating our situation. Best that you not only lock your bedroom door, but take the key to the outside one, too."

The small fire was smaller. Jack crossed the room back to her, stretching out his hand in an offer to help her to her feet. As she took it, the blanket that had been wrapped around her shoulders fell to the floor. He pushed her hair behind her ear.

Oh, God. She was melting and hadn't spent two hours on the couch. The lights were off...not even low. It was crazy, but she wanted to throw her arms around this man and kiss him until he was just as crazy.

Jack, on the other hand, kept her hands firmly gripped in front of his abs. She wasn't really moving without bringing attention to those movements. So she stood there without a word...just like she'd shut herself up earlier.

But there was a lot said in the long, soul-quenching look he gave her. Everything quickened. Her insides literally jumped. Her skin sensitivity to the touch of his thumbs on the backs of her hands skyrocketed.

Was his heart beating as fast as hers? His pulse didn't feel like it. Excitement radiated in his eyes, in the slight upward curve of his lips. He slowly raised his left eyebrow, the gesture that asked more than a paragraph of questioning.

"I'd offer you the TV, but it doesn't pick up anything out here without the internet." His voice was normal—deep and normal. "I'd feel better if you chose the front room with the window instead of the back with the sliding doors."

"Sure." Her voice shook like she'd just finished a mile run.

"Megan, if the SUVs do show up, lock yourself in the main bathroom. It'll slow them down."

"Sure."

"No heroics." He squeezed her hands.

"Sure."

Yeah, that was her. Staring into this gorgeous, dimple-on-his-chin man with abs she couldn't wait to get her hands on. She sounded like someone who knew one word of English, agreeing with everything he said.

Or like someone who wanted to complicate a relationship.

"Well…good night." He pressed the key into her palm. "Don't forget to lock all the doors."

Shoot. He wasn't going to tuck her in after all.

Chapter Ten

Jack closed the cabinet after washing and replacing the plates. He thought about the Murphy bed but decided on the couch. If he moved it to back up against the kitchen island, he had a larger visual range and it could be easier to keep his eyes open.

Coffee. He needed coffee. After that good—but heavy—meal, he needed something with strong caffeine to keep him awake.

The door banged open and he spun, reaching for his nine millimeter.

"What's wrong?" he shouted, chambering a round. He crossed the short distance to Megan and pulled her protectively under one shoulder, pushing her back against the wall. He kept his body between her and whatever threat she'd seen. "Damn glass walls. I shouldn't have brought you here. It's too open."

"Jack. It's fine. I was cold and I'm waiting on

the other half of the house to warm up. It's on a different heater."

He pointed his gun toward the ceiling and stepped to the side. "You can't get under the covers?"

"They're like ice. Seriously. I was about to take a shower, but my toes are blue."

"What are you doing without— Right. You don't have real shoes or socks or other clothes. Let me look around." He pulled the door behind him. The wind was kicking up, blasting through the cypress trees, blasting through him. "No wonder the door slammed against the wall. Shoot, it is cold over here."

Storms like this weren't uncommon. He rubbed his hands together, raiding the dresser until he found socks. Digging through the drawer, he found a thick pair of woolens in the back. Then he looked in the bathroom for extra blankets. "Jackpot."

He carried the socks along with an electric blanket back to the living area. First thing through the door, he plugged the blanket in and draped it around Megan. Then he pulled a chair close to the fire, added some logs and pointed.

"Warm up before you head back over."

"I'm not ready for sleep yet. And I don't think you want my laptop running just in case they're tracing it. Right? So, do the owners have games or something? No movies."

He thought back to the sensual good-night they'd already shared without any contact and agreed. Turning the lights off wasn't safe. He called out the name of old board games in the same closet as the DVDs.

"Oh, oh, oh! Battleship."

Jack set up a card table, then grabbed the game. Megan shivered again and pulled her legs into the oversize chair. He threw the last two logs on the fire, wiping beads of sweat from his forehead. Then he hooked his nine millimeter down his back at his belt.

He took a long route around the house, stepping into the woods and waiting. The wind had turned even chillier with a briskness that smelled like rain. He picked up another armful of logs and verified that all the compartments on his truck were locked.

"I verified that all the pieces were here. You ready to play?"

Jack stuck his backside to the fire and then warmed up his front before sitting in his chair and setting up his board.

They called out letters and numbers until Jack ultimately won. He thought that was it. That the cute state agent would head to bed once she lost. But she didn't. She pulled the pegs from her game pieces and set up again. Resituating herself in her chair and verifying the setting on the electric blanket.

"Why is it that when I'm freezing, I think of ice cream and all the flavors I'd love to be having in front of this fire?"

"Now, that's funny." Jack fanned his T-shirt away from his neck. "I don't know what's wrong with your body's temperature gauge. I'm actually hot."

"Know what would be funnier? Strip Battleship." Megan laughed. "You'd cool off pretty quick that way."

"You'd have to win a game first."

"Oh, now that I've seen your strategy, I think I can pull it off. Or rather, you can pull it off." She laughed more, finding her play on words hilarious.

Pushing his chair away from the table, he said, "I'm going to check outside again and get some more wood if you aren't heading to bed."

"It's a bet, then?" she asked with an overly exaggerated sad face.

"That you can beat me? Sure. But you need to sleep sometime soon. I'll be waking you pretty early to keep watch so I can nap."

"I can take a watch now if you're tired," she offered.

He shook his head. "I'll be gone about twenty

minutes this time. I want to walk to the main road for a look."

"Toss me that pillow, will you?"

He did and left. It actually took him over half an hour to make it to the road, check out a noise from the nearest house and get back inside. The lights were off. His witness—or prisoner or damsel in distress who didn't seem distressed at all—was fast asleep next to the fire.

Careful not to wake her, he gently shut the door, got a bottle of water and put his socked feet near the fire. He sucked the bottle dry, watching Megan sleep. It didn't seem weird or feel strange.

"What time is it?" She stretched her arms from under the blanket. "Wow, you left over an hour ago. Why didn't you wake me up?"

"I was enjoying the fire while I warmed up."

She pushed herself to a sitting position, flipped the electric blanket to low and repositioned her Battleship pieces. "Just in case you peeked while I was asleep." She winked at him with a smile he was coming to appreciate. "You ready to lose your shirt?"

She was kidding, of course. No one ever played strip Battleship. Did they?

They called out the numbers. She took all his ships except one, the smallest. Then in two fatal blows…she'd won.

He stood and stretched, intending to put everything away.

"Not on your life. You lost. What's coming off?"

"You're joking. We agreed that we shouldn't... That it wouldn't be good to get too complicated."

"A bet's a bet, Jack. That's all. No complications. You owe me a piece of clothing." She crossed her arms, not laughing, just summing him up.

She had to be teasing him. "You're kidding."

"Nope."

"But we agreed."

"I believe you made up your mind and dictated. Come on, Jack. No one's coming. If they had followed us, they would be here by now."

"Like at the diner."

"The diner was the perfect example of the SUVs not even knowing who they were chasing. You said several times that no one will think this is where you'd go. Not even your partner knows about this place."

"Building a fire and playing a game or two doesn't put us in danger."

"I hear a big *but* coming, and I'm going to stop you before you say it. You said I could trust you. It's simple, really. Either you're a man of your word or not."

Was this her way of going off on her own as

soon as he was asleep? Would she leave his protection because he didn't follow through on a simple bet?

"Dammit to hell and back." He'd already pulled his boots off. They wouldn't count. He should start with a sock but he unbuttoned his booster-club shirt and slipped it off his shoulders instead.

MEGAN HAD HER fingers crossed that he'd give in and pull his shirt off. He chucked it back to the couch and sat in his chair with a loud huff.

"You're playing a very dangerous game." He pulled out the plastic case with his ships and pegs and began resetting his board, before losing again and removing his undershirt.

She did the same, smashing her lips together to keep from laughing.

It was dangerous because of the attraction. But he'd teased her before sending her to her room. She'd gotten into the bedroom, turned up the heat and immediately found the electric blankct. But then it had dawned on her just how well Ranger Jack MacKinnon had played her like a fiddle.

Strip Battleship was all his fault.

It was her turn to take a long look and appreciate the man in front of her.

Every time he tensed, the muscles in his arms flexed. His chest looked rock solid, as if he hadn't wasted a moment of his workouts. She did feel a little bad when he scooted his chair closer to the fire.

No, not really.

They began their third game. She worked her grid.

"Was this a test?"

"Sort of. But come on. You're a nice guy to gaze at."

He threw his head back and chuckled. "So it's revenge?"

They called out more numbers. He hit a couple of ships and never let up until she was saying, "You sank my battleship."

He leaned back, placing his hands behind his head. His bare chest across the table from her in all its perfection. "Your turn."

"Oh, no. There's no need to take this any further, Jack. I'll head to bed."

"Now you're tired?" He ticktocked a finger at her and made a tsking sound. "Oh, no, lady. You better crank that blanket up to extra high. You're going to need it. Now…something's coming off."

The tight high-school shirt that had restricted her breathing all day could finally come off. In fact, she almost had it over her head when it sort of got stuck. Jack reached across the table and lent her a hand for leverage.

Thank God she'd worn a good bra yesterday.

Barely any lace, just plain, silky and beige. She quickly wrapped herself in the warmth of cotton.

"Are you game for another round?" he asked with a silky edge to his voice.

"Only if I can have that pie you haven't eaten."

"Sure. Help yourself."

She unwrapped her legs and realized she'd have to retrieve the pie without the safety blanket. "I am pretty full."

"Thought so."

They rapidly called the numbers. Each taking a game and each losing a right sock. Then the left. When midnight rolled around, Jack began putting his socks back on.

"Forfeiting?" she asked, secretly relieved.

"Taking care of that pretty little hide of yours." He stomped his second foot into his boot. "I've got to make another round of the perimeter."

"Just remember where we were."

"It's going to be hard to forget in all the cold wind and drizzle sliding down my neck."

"Isn't there a hat or something you could borrow?"

"Better to just get it over with. I won't be long." He backed up to the fire, rubbing his hands up and down his jeans. His gorgeous sculpted chest called out to be touched, but she kept her hands to herself.

"This is as far as we should probably go. It was

fun. The teasing is getting dangerously close to… what did you call it? Oh, yeah. Complications. Dangerously close to complications."

"What? You suddenly don't like complications? Or is it living dangerously that you're hesitant about?"

Living dangerously? "Well, I've been on that radar since rock climbing with my dad. Then it was skydiving and a few flying lessons before I was twenty. Then my parents retired to England, and Mother declared it was her turn. She has him growing prize roses and trimming bushes. Check that—hedges."

"Sounds like a nice life." He nodded.

Was that envy or just agreement?

"It was until the academy. That's when he withdrew his support. He wanted nothing to do with me becoming a cop."

"So why did you?"

She'd answer him just as soon as she could look at his face and not his chest. *My, oh, my.* "I, um… I didn't want to be a cop as much as I wanted to be an investigator. That's why I transferred as soon as I met the TDI requirement."

"At least your dad hasn't got political aspirations and wanted to get elected by pulling you out of deep cover."

"I sense some animosity. Did he really do that?"

She was a little stunned, because she already knew the answer.

"He didn't know where I was located. No one did. When he began his campaign, he wanted me to come home to kick it off. I didn't. The ad people said they wanted to remind people my dad was a family man, the father of a Texas Ranger."

"What happened?"

"Wade saw the commercials. They were pulled almost immediately, but the damage was done. He pretty much saved my life, getting me out of the area I'd been working." He rubbed his heated jeans again.

They'd both cooled off talking about their parents. The only heat left in the room was the actual fire. She gestured for the T-shirt, knowing she wouldn't manage to get it back on with him standing there.

"Ready for this...game to end?"

"I guess it's getting a little late." She shrugged.

"Do you still have the key?" he asked, barely stepping aside to let her stand. He reached around her to move the chair and give her more room.

Wrapped up like a tamale, she wobbled. He caught her. Hands on her hips, his forehead in her chest... Parents or no parents, the fire between them ignited like an arsonist pouring gasoline on a flame.

Jack looked up at her, and the blanket fell away.

His hands slid up her bare midriff, tugging her close. Skin to skin, he dipped that dimpled chin until he could fit his lips over hers. Her hands went around his waist, feeling the contours of the abs she'd been admiring, latching on to his shoulders and drawing him closer to her.

Heat burned her, and she only wanted more. She drank him up like cold water on a sweltering day. As Jack raised his head from hers, his hands stopped their roaming and found their way to her elbows.

"You do like to live dangerously," he whispered. "I'm going to check the perimeter and give you a chance to change your mind."

He grabbed his shirt and darted out the door before she realized her fingers were rubbing her surprised lips.

Complications. Danger. In a moment of clarity, she knew Jack was neither. He was unknown territory, but safe. Very safe.

Chapter Eleven

"I'm telling you she's safe. Hold? Are you serious?"

Wade Hamilton couldn't remember the last time he'd had this much fun. Well, except for the part where Therese kept putting him on hold. The administration part was boring.

Oh, yeah, the last time was probably when the first bullet holes in his truck had been put there. Now he had a matching set to get repaired.

Racing around the countryside. Bullets flying. Tackling a lone suspect to the ground after a scuffle. He couldn't call it a fight, since the guy never connected a punch. He opened the back door of the extended cab, then looked at the man now in his custody.

"I'm not really sure you're clean enough for the seat, man. I mean, I just got it detailed three days ago. Paid extra for the upholstery." He switched the phone to speaker and set it on the bed of the truck, then flipped the seats up.

It was bad enough that this guy had fallen into the mud, forcing Wade to get his boots filthy. There was no way he was letting him ruin his interior. It'd be a different story if Therese would get him a local to come pick him up.

"Man, you're almost more trouble than you're worth. Do you know that?"

"I know that you're a dead man. We're going to cut you into little pieces and feed you to the coyotes." He spit dirt and blood onto the blacktop.

"You think somebody's listening to you?" Wade pointed his finger, drawing a circle to frame his face. "See any bruises forming on my face? I don't think so."

"Wade?" Therese's voice broke from some type of interference. "Are you there?"

"Yeah, I'm *still* here. You give the PD from Enchanted City my locale?"

"They aren't coming."

There was more to the words than just a negative reply. He cut the cocky can't-get-me attitude, tapped the phone off speaker and put it to his ear so the suspect couldn't hear. "What do you mean? Our agreement was—"

"I remember the details of our agreement. I help you get your partner out of one of the deadliest border gangs in America before he's killed, and you owe me."

"I've kept my bargain. I caught your damned bad guy."

"Oh, he's not mine, Wade. *You* need to decide why you arrest him—"

There was such a long pause Wade thought he'd lost the connection. Then he turned to the man he knew was Ronnie Nowland, a convicted felon, and said, "Or *if* I arrest him. Right?"

"You're a sweet kid, Wade. But this is the big leagues. The conversation between us was just a conversation of what-ifs."

"What-ifs? I don't believe you're going to walk away from this guy. He can get you what you want. And what about my partner? He's risking everything to save your girl and doesn't know why. What am I supposed to tell him? What's he supposed to do Monday?"

Silence.

Wade pulled the phone away from his ear, and sure enough, the connection had been lost. Or Therese had simply hung up.

"What the hell am I supposed to do with you now?" He tossed the phone in the front seat and slammed the doors.

"Let me go and I won't cut you until I have my knife back."

"Shut up." Wade paced the length of the truck.

The criminal sucked in air as if to speak.

"Uh-uh," Wade warned. "Shut up or you won't be conscious to think about it."

Idle threat. Wade was limited about what he could do. He hated being beholden to Therese and the people she worked for…whoever they were. Yeah, the people she worked for. A complete unknown.

Wade hadn't stopped to think about who might have been helping him last summer when Jack's father's campaign released the information that he was a Texas Ranger. There was one thing about being a proud papa and using the information. But Jack Sr. knew his son was unavailable for public appearances.

Wade might have let it slip on purpose that he couldn't be pulled from the undercover assignment. He'd never told his partner that had happened. Just like he'd never told his partner how he'd sweet-talked two helicopter pilots into flying in with him in a Navy SEAL rescue move.

Jack had asked, and he'd shrugged as an answer.

"Hey, my hands are starting to cramp."

"Do I care?" Wade continued his pacing and kicking rocks in the predawn hour.

He took a second when he heard an engine. A boat was heading out on a Sunday morning to fish. Common occurrence around Enchanted Oaks,

Seven Points, Log Cabin, Gun Barrel City and all the communities around Cedar Creek Lake.

Hell, now he wasn't certain that Enchanted Oaks had a police department. All these smaller communities might be linked to Henderson County. Maybe he could just call them?

"And say what?"

"That's right. This is police brutality. Just wait until someone comes along and sees me lying in the middle of the road."

Wade dug into the emergency kit in his back seat until he found the cheap duct tape. He held it in one hand and pulled the end with the other, ripping off enough to wrap around the convict. "I did warn you to be quiet."

He wrapped it completely around the man's head—hair and all.

But the guy was right about one thing. He couldn't be lying in the street when the community got up for church…or fishing, which would be happening soon.

Wade glanced at his watch. He needed a decision and quick.

"How do I get myself into these messes and why do I normally need Jack to get me out of them?"

Ronnie Nowland tried to talk through the tape. Wade ignored him. He leaned across the front seat and retrieved his badge from under the passenger seat. He'd left his weapons at home. With all the shooting, he might have actually shot back.

He unlocked the built-in gun case in the side of his truck. Both he and Jack had had them installed at the same time. It was a safe way they could carry weapons. Even in a state that allowed open carry. He'd grown up where his uncle had a gun rack and carried rifles openly…everywhere.

Storing Ronnie's weapons in the built-in gun safe, he bounced the .45 in the palm of his hand a couple of times but dropped it inside. He didn't need to share his personal reason for getting Ronnie off the street. His reason was that he was a Texas Ranger and saw a weapon. A parole violation was reason enough to arrest him.

Would it really matter to the higher-ups if he reacted to something he saw without calling it in? Probably. Later. He could deal with it later, too.

"I'm going to remove the tape and you're going to answer my questions."

Lying on his side, Ronnie made a finger gesture behind his back.

"You did that even in cuffs. Good for you. But I don't really care. I need an answer, and you're it." He ripped the tape from Ronnie's mouth and hair, ignoring his scream. "Yeah, I bet that hurt."

He might be talking like a smart-ass, but his eyes searched the perimeter for either Ronnie's pals or a resident. Still alone.

"My friend sent me to you. So I'm pretty sure you know who hired you to take out Megan Harper."

"I ain't telling you—"

"Mind your manners, Ronnie. I'm getting a little tired of being called names. Just give me the ones I want."

"No way." He shook his head and spit red dirt mixed with blood from his split lip. "They'll kill me, man."

"You don't get it, Ronnie. No one knows we're here, and there's lots of things I can do at a place like this."

"You wouldn't. You're a ranger. You guys don't even pick your noses in public."

Wade knelt next to his prisoner, laughing as crazily as he could. "That's funny, and most of the time I'd agree. But you see, today I'm just a guy trying to prevent your friends from killing mine." He pulled Ronnie's ear toward the sky. "You get one more chance to tell me before that knife of yours takes off a slice."

"You threw it in the lake."

"Did I?"

Wade walked to the truck and removed his utility knife. All he had to do was let Ronnie *think* he'd kept the man's weapon. He just had to *think* Wade would use it. But the parole-breaking convict/suspect/prisoner had one thing right... Texas

Rangers were squeaky-clean. He was no exception under ordinary conditions.

He might play his hunches more than his partner, but they both knew when to rein in the rule-breaking.

But this ranger was also desperate. He had no idea where his partner had gone. No idea if he'd been compromised or captured. No idea why Megan Harper was so important to Therese or the men this fella was working for.

"Ronnie, there's only one thing I hate in life… that's being left out of the fun." He showed the tip of the utility knife, and Ronnie's eyes got huge. "You need to know that I'm willing to do whatever it takes to find my partner. Even pick my nose."

MEGAN ROLLED OVER, wrapped in pleasant warmth. Sunshine streamed through the flowy white curtains. She'd had the most delicious dream last night about playing strip Battleship.

She popped straight up in bed, the covers—including the electric blanket—dropping to her waist. Thank goodness she was still in her bra and panties. The realization that she was only grateful because she had no memory of what had happened was sobering. She must have fallen asleep and Jack had brought her to bed.

Alone. *Joy.*

It seemed the sunshine was a momentary thing.

Rain pelted the ground outside the window. The wind shoved the trees from side to side. A true storm had begun. She searched the room for her clothes.

Facing Jack…without clothes… She threw the covers over her head and wanted to travel back in time a week. Shoot, maybe she should go back before any of the Dallas fires had landed on her desk.

"Oh. My. Gosh. That's it."

Jumping up, she pulled the closet open, searching for a shirt.

"Come on, come on, come on. There has to be an old shirt that— Perfect." An old red flannel man's shirt was just the softness she needed when she pushed her arms through the sleeves and rolled up the cuffs.

A quick search of the dresser led her to a pair of yoga pants. No pockets for the key to the double-bedroom side of the house made her stuff it inside her bra. It should be safe from Jack there.

Check that. Safe from *her*.

The strong man seemed interested but obviously could restrain himself much better than she could. Lightning broke through the clouds, quickly followed by thunder.

She looked to either side of the covered porch. Walls of water from the downpour made it impossible to see twenty feet away from the house. "Great—I'm stuck in a lifeboat."

"A lifeboat?" a deep voice questioned.

She should have jumped, but his voice was a part of her memory now. It triggered security and...well, other things she couldn't admit.

"Yeah. I might be glad to be alive, but the limitations will make me a bit stir-crazy."

Jack shrugged. "I guess that does sort of sound like a lifeboat. Although we can leave anytime we want, Megan. It's just rain."

Backing his words was perfectly timed lightning and instant thunder.

"Man, that was close." She was about to close the door behind her when the realization that he was soaked hit her over the head. "You should take a hot shower and get out of those wet clothes."

"I was thinking about that. Do you mind?"

The mist from the downpour filled the air, and man, did she want that hot shower, too! Quickly stepping aside to avoid physical contact, she bolted for the living area, hearing Jack's laughter echo around the porch.

Food. She checked cabinets and found soup, chili, canned veggies, bins of healthy cereal, protein bars, dried prunes. "Yuck." The refrigerator and freezer were stocked with things that wouldn't go bad.

Why was Jack wet? She stared into the freezer,

looking at the uncooked chicken and steak. He'd checked the perimeter again. *Even in this weather.* Back and forth, her eyes shifted to the washer and dryer. She'd looked through all the clothes available in the bedrooms. Jack's frame was much bigger than the available clothes. He'd never fit.

Even into stretchy yoga pants. The thought made her laugh.

Before she could change her mind, she darted across to the bath. She heard the shower and Jack's deep voice talking to himself. It wasn't singing… just running through threat scenarios and escape routes. She plucked the pile of soaked clothing from the sink and gently pulled the doors back.

She started the washer and threw everything inside. Her things could use a quick wash, too. So she shimmied out of her underclothes and back into the flannel and stretchy nylon. The key she left on the counter.

Then she was back staring at dried prunes, potato flakes and creamed corn. She'd just switched to staring into the refrigerator when the door burst open.

"I have a good idea why you took my clothes, but it's not happening. Where are they?"

She didn't turn around. Lightning. Thunder. Door slam. And then she could hear the spin cycle on the small washer kick in. Apparently, so did Jack, because he wasn't raising his voice any longer.

Megan closed the refrigerator and slowly turned around to face her protector. His bare feet were wet from crossing the porch, the hair on his legs still plastered to his muscular calves. The plain white towel held together with one tuck hung low on his hips. Tanned skin covered the abdominal six-pack she admired. His shaggy hair still dripped onto his superbly built shoulders.

And, good Lord, his dimpled chin predominating from the frown on his face just gave her shivers of excitement.

"That wasn't a good idea," he finally said.

Nope, he was wrong. She thoroughly disagreed. Washing his clothes for him was one of the best ideas she'd ever had.

Chapter Twelve

It wasn't normal for anyone to come to the office on Sunday. Alvie Balsawood accepted that today was different. Everyone connected to this case was either being interviewed or helping with Megan's files. He hadn't been called as most of these morons had, but they'd allowed him in the building anyway.

Not having received a call for interrogation proved—to him at least—that he'd covered any connections to Megan. He mentally shrugged. Knowing he was good did little to locate her. All of his calculations couldn't have accounted for the unknown factor of someone offering her assistance.

Megan Harper was essentially alone. Her parents resided in Bristol, and after all the traveling in their lives, they didn't even venture on the train to London. Oh, yes, he'd done his research. And he'd done his calculations more than once.

The chances for Megan to survive the encounter at the Austin airport had been higher than he liked. But drugging her before she'd gotten on the plane should have lowered those odds. No research or informant had let him know about two wild-card Texas Rangers coming to her rescue.

Why were they involved?

That was the question holding all the answers. If he could figure out how they'd stumbled onto Megan's dilemma, perhaps he could either predict their actions or at least discover where they were hiding with his research.

Jack MacKinnon had obviously been sent by his partner to the airport. But how had Wade Hamilton become involved in the first place?

"Hey, Alvie. They called you in, too?"

He nodded and stopped, ready with his prepared explanation of why he'd decided to work on a Sunday and offer his services to the authorities. But the man who asked had already moved on with a wave at the woman in the next cubicle.

Walking a little faster, he rounded the corner and went past the restrooms and water fountain to the back of all the offices, where his was located. The opposite side of the building from the up-and-coming, ever-popular Miss Harper. But fortunately, today it was also the farthest from the activity and investigators.

The information he needed would have been

flagged as suspicious if he'd gone anywhere other than here at TDI. But here, if caught...

That thought made him laugh. He'd never be caught. The searches might be flagged from somewhere, but here in his report they were disguised as part of what was already going on.

Logical. Methodical.

His two best traits.

The men working around him seemed devoted to upholding the law. Cracking their evaluations within the Texas DPS was a little harder, and before he knew it, several hours had passed. But of course, no one had bothered him tucked away in his corner.

A few additional searches yielded everything he needed on the two Rangers. Known associates, their service history, credit history, places of residence, education, family, purchases. Aw... yes. Purchases led him to...a ring.

He was back on track and could leave now. Electronically, he'd hidden his path. Physically, some of his coworkers jokingly referred to him as the invisible man. He just wasn't noticeable. How little did they know that their description was true?

But that would all change.

Soon.

The elimination of Megan Harper would clear his path, and then people would take note. Years from now, he'd be a required case study for the analysts coming after him.

By then he wouldn't be invisible.

People with money never were.

Chapter Thirteen

"What's for lunch?"

Jack had been waiting on his jeans to dry for the past half hour. They were close. Had to be close. Normally, he'd be comfortable watching a movie with a beautiful woman at his side. Not today.

Every half hour that ticked by had the potential to bring unwanted guys driving black SUVs to their doorstep. He couldn't continue to sit here, naked except for a towel and a wolf blanket.

Megan wasn't naked, but the yoga pants left nothing—absolutely nothing—to his imagination. The flannel shirt was too big, but it didn't matter. She'd tied the shirttail to where it fell just below her breasts, perfectly outlining the firm…

"I found popcorn in the freezer. Want me to microwave it?"

The temperature had dropped to below sixty outside and he would be standing in the cold rain again if he didn't restrict his thoughts. He wiped the sweat beaded on his forehead. Staying away from this woman was the hardest thing he'd done.

The house seemed safe. He'd checked the perimeter every hour since they'd arrived. No one seemed to be around. No new tire tracks on the main road connecting the three houses on it.

Yeah, it seemed like they had time to wait out the threats.

The nervousness tingling throughout his body was totally due to Megan, who couldn't sit still. She seemed as antsy as him.

He purposely drew in a deep breath and released it silently and slowly to calm his body. "There's lots of stuff in there to fix if you want real food."

"You mean there are lots of ingredients. I don't see any food to heat up at all."

He threw his head back and laughed. Then stood, holding the towel together as the blanket stayed on the couch. "You don't cook?"

"You do?"

"Yeah. I'm not bad, either."

She bowed, and her breasts swayed, free from the entrapment of a bra. "By all means…the kitchen is yours."

He tugged one-handed at the throw. It was firmly caught between the couch cushions, maybe even on his gun that he'd pushed there earlier. He left it. The kitchen island would be between them if his makeshift kilt came unhooked.

"If you feel like you need a cape, I can do that for you. But I promise to keep my distance and not attack you with my claws." She gestured with her fingers in a catlike motion.

Ten minutes and he'd have pants. But did he really trust a woman who'd been suggesting they have sex? Did he trust that he was still sane after turning her down?

Strip Battleship, one of the sexiest kisses he'd had and now naked chef… Damn, he was *not* including this in any report.

Megan walked to the south side of the couch, and Jack chose the longer north side. He almost stopped to yank on damp underwear, but his guest would give him an even harder time about his timidity.

"What are you afraid of?" she'd asked after his shower. "It's just skin."

Right. Just his skin if headquarters caught wind of it. He'd be skinned alive, and that wouldn't be a pretty picture.

"Just have a seat and finish the movie."

Not to his surprise, she picked up the remote, switched off the television and sat on a bar stool at the island where he was working. The towel was hooked together at his hip. It wasn't the first time in the past two hours that he'd wished for a clothespin, a safety pin or even a paper clip. Something to keep the thing closed.

"You're not going to finish the movie?"

"And miss this show? Absolutely not." She winked.

"You're really enjoying the compromising situation you've put me in."

"This isn't a compromise, Ranger MacKinnon. Would you feel more comfortable if I call you Little Jack?"

He removed some frozen catfish, dropped the plastic bag in a bowl of water and placed it in the microwave to defrost. "We can skip that conversation. I think you picked up real fast that it's not my favorite nickname."

Careful not to show everything God gave him, he knelt and brought up a deep fryer. Oil, cornmeal, a little flour, salt and pepper—they all came from the pantry while Megan remained on her stool.

Her rye-colored green eyes seemed to be watching him intently each time he dared to glance up at her. He dropped the first piece into the heated oil.

"What kind of fish is that?"

"Catfish."

"You look like you've done that a lot."

"My mom hated fish. When I caught it, I had to learn real fast how to fry it up. Deep fryers make it a lot easier—less grease spatters." He sliced the next fish and dropped it in the cornmeal. "If I had milk, I'd mix us up some hush puppies."

"I've never had catfish. I've seen it on menus, but I've had fried fish all over the world. It's not my favorite." She scrunched up her nose, making a face that was meant to be unflattering toward fish.

All he could do was smile.

"There you go again. If you want me to stop making advances, then stop showing off the dimples."

"I wasn't trying."

"Oh, I know. That's why it's so appealing." She leaned forward, swaying breasts and all.

"It smells good. All fried food does as long as the oil isn't terribly old." She sat back again. "You see, I've listened to a couple of cooking shows in my time."

Why was he fighting the 100 percent cuteness in front of him? His career. At some point he'd have to recount what happened between them. But damn—a buzzer went off in his head, making him realize it wasn't the risk to his career... it was sharing any part of her with Wade or the other Rangers in Company B. Two days around this woman, and he wanted her all to himself.

Okay, the buzzer was buzzing again.

"I'll check it. Your hands are all gooey."

Dryer...that was the dryer buzzer, not his brain.

He might be thinking about things a whole lot more than he needed to be. Things like sleeping with Megan.

He might not make it alone with her in the house of his almost fiancée one more night. Hell, he might not make it through lunch.

EVERYTHING WAS DRY except Jack's jeans. If she didn't let him feel the dang things, he'd accuse her of lying. So she pulled everything out—except the jeans—and folded them. She was comfortable in the flannel shirt and in no rush to put her borrowed jeans back on.

"Are you sure I shouldn't just eat another granola bar?" she teased, starting the dryer for another twenty minutes.

He harrumphed under his breath and reached for paper plates on the top shelf. She covered her mouth to keep her reaction to the bottom of his bum to herself. She wouldn't mind catching a glimpse of that again.

"Looks like the rain is stopping. We aren't going to be trapped down here or anything. I mean, the truck can still make it up that driveway, right?"

"I promise."

He dished up the catfish on paper plates and placed a white substance next to it.

"Ketchup?" she asked, deliberately insulting the

chef. "Sorry, just teasing. Fair warning, though. I've used ketchup my whole life. It was always available at the commissary, and Mom always bought it by the case."

"Tartar sauce first. If you don't like it then use the entire bottle." He pulled it from the refrigerator, setting it next to her plate. He popped the can on an energy drink for himself. He tipped it toward her, silently asking if she wanted one as well.

"No, thanks. I think I'm going to have a hard enough time sleeping tonight as it is."

"Careful—it's still hot." He turned the can up, taking a giant gulp.

"Don't I know it?" She was staring at his biceps and his chest flexing, but quickly dived into the cornmeal-covered fillet, ignoring his warning.

Six pieces of fish later, she had a new favorite fried food and loved tartar sauce. She began clearing away the ingredients while Jack changed into his clothes. She'd tried to talk him out of it, since he was determined to go walk the perimeter and was certain to get everything soaked again.

The man was a strong-minded protection machine and she really, really liked him.

"All kidding aside, Megan," he said, pulling his T-shirt over his head as he reentered from the half bath. "Get dressed. I don't think we should hang around here too much longer."

"Copy that."

He looked up, that questioning gaze she admired catching her by surprise. "No arguments? No jokes about a perfectly good bed going to waste?"

"I never said that, but now that you're mentioning it…"

"It'll take me fifteen minutes. Tops. Be ready."

"Do you think I could borrow the rubber boots?"

He paused at the back door. "Yeah. I'll be calling up the owners and asking them for the cleaning bill."

"Be sure to ask for a receipt. I can probably expense that…eventually."

He laughed and shut the door behind him. She swiped her clothes off the dryer and quickly changed. That sense of urgency his voice had held rubbed off. Maybe they had been too complacent and now that the rain had let up, it was time to move on.

She finished the cleanup as best she could. The grease stayed in the deep fryer, since it was still warm and she had no idea what to do with it anyway. She snagged some protein granola bars and two more of the energy drinks along with some bottled water. She stashed them all in her laptop bag and was folding the last blanket when she heard it.

Something.

In all the lack of noise that this place had… something that didn't belong really stood out. She placed her back to the fireplace and searched all the dead bolts. They were all locked. She needed to make a quick decision.

Either someone was already watching her and if she acted weird—as in hiding—they'd know she knew they were there. Or she took a risk that they hadn't gotten close enough to see her and hid. She spied the key on the granite counter.

Yes, the best place to be was probably on the bedroom side of this house. She could make a run for it, wielding the fireplace poker, but by crossing the porch she was at a superhigh risk. She searched the cabin for a second weapon.

"You're panicking for nothing, Megan," she whispered. It was probably another deer banking into one of the cute statues of frogs out front. To make that determination, she had to expose her position in a window.

Think like Dad. What would he do?

Assess the situation. She was vulnerable, that was true. But what had Jack mentioned? In order to get to the house, the SUV guys would have to approach from the road—double windows on the north side. They might be able to see her pass by but wouldn't know exactly where she was if she stayed on the kitchen side of the room.

The entire south wall was glass panels that

pushed aside to open the back of the house. Absolutely no protection, but that was her way out of the house. The creek. The nonpath that they'd have to follow her down.

She slipped the flip-flops down the back of her shirt. She couldn't afford to lose them. Then she pulled on the rubber boots and as casually as possible—hyperventilating the entire way—made it to the area between the sink and stove. It was one thing to talk big and relax when there was no actual threat. Quite another to think clearly when one might—

Strike that.

Another bang and a curse. There was no longer any doubt. Someone who hadn't walked outside every hour since they'd been there was outside and had just tripped over something. In other words, she and Jack had company.

Chapter Fourteen

Megan stayed put. She didn't have much cop experience to go on. She'd only been in a patrol car a short time. But she did have her father's training embedded in her DNA. If there was one thing she'd learned about a dangerous situation, it was that there could only be one leader.

She might disagree with Jack, but he was the one with the gun and the plan. He was outside, which was an advantage. He probably had more details about these men than she did crouched down behind a granite counter.

Even the granite island didn't protect her completely. Everything reflected in this house of glass. The man who stumbled found his way to the main door. He tested the knob.

Megan slipped the laptop shoulder strap off. She gripped the fireplace poker with both hands and waited.

The door being kicked in echoed everywhere.

She was sure everyone sneaking through the woods heard it. Still bent behind the island, she went to the end, watching the guy in the window reflection. One man ran toward her, gun out, yelling. When he was two steps from her, she stood and swung the fireplace poker with all her might, hitting the hot grease pot onto the man's middle.

The gun flew. The man screamed. This time in pain and retreat out the door he'd entered.

Megan stayed behind the island and used the poker to grab the gun and stuck it in her laptop bag. She slipped the strap back over her head, ready to leave.

The back doorknob moved. She wouldn't allow herself to panic. She watched, listened, tried to stop the rush of adrenaline from taking control of her nerves.

"Megan. You okay?"

Jack!

He didn't have a key. She slid across the tile floor, unsure about what to do. Open or not? Did they have a gun to his head? And if they did, would she let him be shot to save her own life?

Staying out of the line of vision through the front windows, she scooted to where the door would be in front of her. She turned the dead bolt, then the knob, then raised the poker, ready to clobber the next enemy. The door opened, and Jack rolled through.

"Five men—or four and one woman. Some are the same I spied at the diner," he panted, catching his breath. "Main roads and driveway are covered. All but one are still about two hundred yards away from the house."

"And the one who broke the front door?"

"Unconscious." He held up a hand radio and smiled.

"Looks like we'll need to split the cleaning bill. Sorry 'bout the mess."

"Not a problem. They're understanding…friends. We need to move. Looks like you're ready."

"You're the slowpoke."

"Right. I forgot." He crouched, hand on the door, ready to open it for them to leave.

"Just think, less than an hour ago, you were cooking with a towel." She laughed.

"Yeah, the timing hasn't been missed by me." He turned the knob, waiting. "Remember, there are three steps down. Stick close to the side of the house. Then there's a thicker group of trees to your left before a sharp drop down to the creek. Don't look back. Don't wait on me. Got it?"

"Check."

She hadn't noticed that his other hand still held his gun. He lifted the corner of his mouth. She knew he'd been using his dimples deliberately.

"Ready? Remember…don't look back. Just keep going."

He pushed the door open. She left first, following the exact path he'd laid out inside. She listened to him about not looking back until she reached the drop-off. At that point she needed to know if he was coming right after her or fighting.

"Move it!"

Behind her. She was a climber, used to plans and safety ropes. But this was more of an unplanned tumble down a rocky mud slide. The trees were like prickly pear. The shallow roots gave way when she tried to use them as an anchor.

The fireplace poker that she'd carried out without thinking came in handy and stopped her slipping several times. Jack was above her, then to the side. He paused more than once, telling her to keep going.

She hit the rock creek bank, slipping to her butt, but there was no time to worry about cuts, bruises or tailbones. She was surprised that the oversize rubber boots were still on her feet.

"Stay close to this bank," Jack said above her. "Remember the plan."

Continue down the creek until they made it to a ranch. It was the longer way, and their pursuers in the SUVs would hopefully think they had chosen the other way.

The boots were like giant plungers into the mud, catching and sinking. After pulling them from the muck twice, she left them there. Jack's feet hitting the rocks was the only sound she heard during her pause. She took a step with her shoeless foot.

"Wait. Throw me the boots." She did. "Now move it. Fast. Through the water. You need to get around that bend in the next two minutes."

Easier said than done.

The creek was shallow but freezing. She tried not to think about it, drawing on the rush of adrenaline that had hit her system. There were shouts above her. Evidently her two minutes were up. The quickest way around the bend was on the other side. It was all rock on the limestone side of the bluff, broken limestone at the bottom. This side was complete mud.

Listen to the leader kept playing through her mind. But which instruction was more important? Getting around the bend and out of sight in two minutes. She ran across the creek, avoiding a deep hole at the last second. She swung her black laptop case above her head, making her realize that her red flannel shirt would be eye-catching against the white limestone.

Taking a huge risk, she made it to the wall, balanced the bag on a rock, pulled the shirt over her head and stuffed it in the outside zipper. Now on dry and rocky ground, she could run.

She heard voices and plastered herself under a rock overhang. Once the voices had drifted farther upstream, she resumed her run, wondering with every step if Jack was having any success.

AFTER MAPPING THE perimeter of the house almost every hour for the past day, Jack was pretty damn familiar with the ruts and holes where trees had fallen. But the riverbank...not so much. He found the first real mud hole and stuck the rubber boots into it.

Then he climbed again. Definitely not his favorite thing. And definitely crazy hard in the mud. He slid more than he climbed or pulled his way back to a steep incline west of the house.

Just as he was about to rest his weary arms, he heard shouts that they'd found the boots. Two men passed five feet in front of him. He held his breath. He was in no shape to fight after that climb. The men cut back toward the house.

Dammit! This is taking longer than I thought it would.

There was no way to catch up with Megan along the creek. Crossing it wasn't an option. Even if he could mentally force himself to climb the hundred-foot bluff, the limestone was slick from the rain and groundwater seepage from above. That left him one choice.

Driving.

His truck was next to the house. His odds of making it weren't very good. They couldn't be.

And that was why it would work. The SUV guys wouldn't be expecting it.

It was slow moving, circling wide so he wouldn't be heard. Most of the noise was at the creek. A couple of them seemed to be close to the house. He had seen the SUVs from a distance and had no idea if someone had been left with each vehicle.

Once he climbed into his cab, there was no turning back. There was only one way to guarantee that they couldn't follow—he would have to ram their vehicles into the ditch on either side of the one-lane road. He wasn't looking forward to the body-shop repair bill.

The deer guard on the front would help. Next time he saw Wade, he'd force him to take back his statement of how it was for all show and had no benefits. He made it to the truck, using the key to silently unlock the door and built-in storage container where he kept his DPS-issued vest. He didn't bother to put it on correctly.

He got in the truck with his loaded weapons stuffed in his belt and the radio dropped down the front of his T-shirt. He couldn't risk that it would fly somewhere during the crash. Then he doubled the vest between him and the door to block someone shooting at him.

No seat belt. He needed to move fast if this thing went sideways. He switched on the ignition and rolled all the windows down. When he cranked the engine, he heard shouts. But he didn't have to worry about the guys behind him.

Just those in front.

Hitting the gas, he bounced up the driveway. Splashes from the puddles flew inside the cab…a necessary evil when you needed to fire a weapon. He kept his eyes glued to the road, or what little of it hadn't been washed out. He kept his foot on the gas instead of braking to turn onto the road connecting the homes through here.

One of the SUVs was parked across the driveway. Jack T-boned the passenger side. Between the dark overcast sky, the shade of the towering trees and the tinted windows, Jack had no way of knowing if there was a shooter still inside the vehicle. He threw the truck in Reverse. Then he went forward, stepping on the gas and ramming the SUV a second time. This hit sent the front of the vehicle into the weeds.

"One down. One to go."

MEGAN HUGGED THE laptop bag to her chest, shivering in thigh-deep water that she wanted out of more than she wanted to escape the creeps making her run through it. *Where the hell is Jack?*

There had been a lot of shouts just a few minutes before she plunged into a very open spot along the creek. There was just enough light to see the sinkholes and avoid them. Otherwise, her laptop would have been toast more than once.

A crash echoed along the bluff, stopping her as she took the last step onto the sandy bank.

Metal on metal, glass breaking, shouting. Another crash. Shots fired.

"Jack."

Don't stop. Don't look back. Keep going no matter what.

The shouts were far away and the words indistinguishable. Whatever Jack had done, he'd successfully drawn the men away from her.

If he was in the truck escaping, then he had a plan of where they'd meet up. She had no choice—she had to push forward. But her legs just weren't moving as quickly. Not only was she tired, she was cold and her feet were numb. Not to mention sliced in several places from sharp rocks.

She had to rub her feet and put on the flip-flops—Jack's sister's shoes.

Shots rang out again. Rapidly. Whoever was firing this time wasn't missing. She heard round after round connect with metal. Another crash. Tires spinning. Metal on metal yet again.

He had to be hitting them deliberately. Disabling them? Making it impossible to follow? She could only guess. Shots continued. They were closer to her, even though the shouting had stopped.

Move your legs, Megan.

Her dad wasn't there, but she heard his voice. It was on one of the hardest, longest climbs he'd taken her on. And toward the top, her body had given out. Or at least she thought it had. But her dad told her to move her left, then her right. Hand over hand, foot over foot.

She'd finished the climb one step at a time.

Like now.

Right foot. Left. Right. Left.

One step, then another.

The water shifted sidcs and so did she, avoiding it when possible, making more progress downstream. Far enough away that there weren't any echoes of shouting or bullets flying.

Jack MacKinnon had saved her life…again.

It began to rain again in earnest. First in small sprinkles, then in sheets, complete with lightning and thunder. Running through the water couldn't possibly be the safest place, but there was no way she could be seen from the bluff above. She saw chairs and a deck, but no lights.

The empty house. She'd had the conversation with Jack about using a phone line. There weren't any. The price one paid for living in practical isolation. So there was no help at thc top of that hill. She slogged on.

Right. Left. Right. Left. Sometimes she had to

lift her foot to make the next step. The next beat of her escape.

She must be delirious. She wiped the rain from her eyes and blinked. But yeah, sitting in the middle of the creek was a white pickup, and it looked like Jack was walking along the bank.

"Megan," he called. "Come here."

She turned to him but couldn't move. If he was a mirage, he was a pretty good one. He lifted her into his warm arms, carrying her back to his truck.

"Damn, woman! You're like ice. Where's your shirt?"

"In…in…in the…"

"Shh, honey. I got ya now. Everything's okay."

They'd done the impossible.

It got dark quickly in a Hill Country thunderstorm. When she warmed up enough that her lips were no longer blue, she asked where they were going.

"Dallas. It's time to find out exactly what's going on."

Thank God.

Chapter Fifteen

The truck was a wreck. Literally. At least they were alive. Jack needed another vehicle before continuing the five-hour drive to Dallas. The windshield had three bullet holes, and he was surprised it hadn't shattered.

"Ouch. My toes are stinging like hornets are attacking them."

"Good—you're defrosting." Jack was certain her core temperature had dropped, but there wasn't a damn thing he could do about it.

"Where's my laptop?"

"Back seat. Why?"

She disengaged her seat belt, dropped the passenger seat back and turned until she grabbed the bag. He heard a zipper and saw a flash of red-and-black flannel. He'd almost forgotten that she wasn't wearing a shirt.

"I can't believe that the inside of this thing is still dry. Man, I came close to dousing it a couple

of times. I'd be lost without that laptop and external drive. Everything is on there." She stretched
her arms through the armholes and brought the
seat back into place. She wedged the black bag at
her feet and opened more pouches.

"Water or an energy drink?"

"What?"

"Aren't you thirsty? I brought drinks. Add it to
my cleaning tab."

"How in the hell can you be making me laugh?
Now?" He didn't understand it, but he was. Before pouring semi-hot oil on one of their attack-
ers, she'd thought to pack snacks.

She laughed, too, popping the tab on a can.
"Here. I'm not sure. Maybe we're both giddy with
relief or something just as obnoxious. I'm sure you
need this. Drink."

He did. She handed him a granola bar, wrap-
ping paper peeled back. His insides weren't shaking as much…just the truck.

"Dammit, I messed the front end up. There's no
way we're driving this thing all the way to Dallas."

"I think it's time for a phone call. What about
you?" She was already retrieving the phones.

"First thing we do is get somewhere and listen
to the messages. A town, preferably with a police
station. If something does start up, you go into
protective custody. Agreed?"

"Sounds reasonable." Megan set the phones in the cup holders. "You sound pretty confident that the SUVs won't be following us. I'm sorry about your truck."

She took napkins from the glove box and stuffed them into the bullet holes where water was streaming in through.

"You should see the other guy," he joked. "There's silver tape in the emergency kit. That might help."

Megan repeated the steps she'd used to retrieve her bag, found the tape and stopped the water spray through the windshield. Then she curled up and fell asleep about five minutes down the road.

He was tempted to turn his phone on and call Wade. Private words, calmly spoken, that wouldn't wake Megan. But he'd wait. It was smarter to be in a place where they could get help immediately.

He hooked Megan's long hair around her ear. His fingers felt how cold she still was. *Damn.* He cranked the heater up another notch, gladly wiping the sweat off his face if it meant Megan got warm. She should have shed her wet jeans, but they were still stuck to her legs. That must be keeping her cold.

He couldn't wait long to get her temperature back to normal. They wouldn't be good to anybody—especially each other—if they were stiff or sick.

If his memory was right, the next superstore was at Highway 1 and 290. The thing about heading that direction was that he might as well deliver Megan to headquarters. Talk about the safest thing to do...

But he wanted to finish this. Hell, he wanted to begin whatever it was he'd become involved with. Clothes, another vehicle...there was one place he could get both and where he knew the chief of police and the mayor.

Hell, he was the mayor this week.

"It'll be risky." He'd have to verify that no one was watching his sister's place on the ranch.

Feeling the coolness of Megan's cheek...it was their best bet. Once there, he'd have access to a ranch hand's phone that no one would be monitoring.

So when it came time to turn east toward Austin, Jack kept to the smaller roads. The reduced speed as he skirted the Colorado River made it easier to steer. It took longer, but someone had thought ahead and given him an energy drink.

Lightning danced across the sky. He turned on the radio and kept sneaking looks at Megan. She didn't wake when they pulled into the back lot at the Liberty Hill Police Station. He left the truck—

and the heater—running while he banged on the back door until the deputy opened.

"Hey, Little Jack. Whatcha doin' out here? Hell of a storm today. You look like— Good Lord, what happened to your truck?"

"Yeah, we hit some water. Hydroplaned into a tree. It was pretty bad. I was wondering if I could borrow your phone, Aaron."

"Sure. Come on inside."

"No, thanks. My girlfriend's asleep. I just need to call Gillic real fast."

"It's on the charger. I'll be right back." The door swung closed.

Jack kicked some rocks and thought about whom to involve. He needed Gillie. But they'd found them in Wimberley. And that was a place without any direct connection to him. Odds were pretty good that whoever was after Megan was already monitoring his sister's phone.

Aaron returned, extending the cell to him. "Dad blast, it's colder out here than a milk cow's teat. You want a jacket? I have a couple in Lost and Found."

Before he could say no, thanks, Aaron was gone again. It gave Jack the opportunity to scroll through the deputy's list of contacts. He called one of Gillie's neighbors, who called her and asked her to call Aaron.

The phone rang just as the deputy brought out an old bomber jacket.

"Gillie?"

"What's gone wrong, Jack? I've been worried sick."

He shook his head and waved off the offer of the coat. "Is anyone watching your house?"

"And why would I be under surveillance?"

He turned away from Aaron and walked to the back of the truck, noticing that the damage wasn't nearly as bad as he'd thought. "Listen to me, Gilleth Anne. I need you. No questions right now. Okay?"

He explained what she needed to do to verify no one was following her before she could come for them. He handed the phone back to Aaron. "Thanks, man. I know this all seems strange, but will you keep it to yourself for a while?"

"Does this mean you owe me a favor?" Aaron asked.

"Sure—anything."

"I want to drive the Model T in the parade Saturday."

"The Model T that my dad drives? The mayor? The same guy who was just elected to the Senate?"

"Yeah. I've always wanted to drive that thing." Aaron tossed him the jacket. "You should keep that."

"Jack's going to be seriously ticked, but I'll find another place for him."

"Dad blast, Little Jack. I didn't think you'd say yes. This must be pretty serious." He leaned in a bit closer. "It must be Texas Rangers stuff. Everyone said that's the only thing that would take you away from the homecoming meeting."

"That's right." *Sort of.* But if it kept the phone calls to a minimum, he'd let Aaron run with it. "Think you could move the truck to a body shop tomorrow?"

"Hey, anything you need. You're letting me drive the Model T." Aaron slapped his arm. "I'm heading inside. Want some coffee or something?"

His dad would just have to understand and take his place in the back seat. Come to think about it, that was a good place for him. Telling him about it might take a little last-minute maneuvering. At least Jack hoped to be back to tell him.

"I'm good. I'll leave the keys under the mat. Thanks, man."

"Anything for the Rangers." He waved and went inside.

Waved?

Jack looked in the truck and saw Megan was awake. She smiled and waved.

"Time for our phone calls?" she asked once he was inside. "By the way, where are we?"

"Liberty Hill. My sister's on her way."

"Look, I like your sister and I definitely appreciate her jeans—" she slapped the denim, then rubbed her hands together "—but don't you think her coming with us is a little dangerous?"

"I'm not bringing her. We're borrowing a ranch hand's car, making some phone calls and getting you some dry clothes."

She rubbed her fingers across her lips, thinking. "Is there a sandwich in there, too? Or are you frying fish again?"

"After your attempt at cleaning up? No way."

Laughing again. She had him making jokes about the men after her. And she hadn't questioned his decision. Megan was smart—not because she agreed with him. Well, that wasn't the only reason. No, he could see her mind working. She weighed the options and agreed that he'd chosen the right path.

There were plenty of times when she'd disagreed and they'd talked it through.

"What day is it?"

"Sunday." He raised the bottle of water she'd handed him.

"Are you sure? I feel like I've slept with you more than just a couple of nights."

Water shot up his nose at her deliberate double entendre. She'd really slept around him or with him in a truck. And the lack of sex hadn't been for a lack of trying. He laughed. He couldn't help it.

It was the strangest thing. He'd laughed more with Megan in two days than he had with the woman he'd wanted to marry. It was the first time in two years that he was thankful Toni had turned him down.

"Thanks. I needed that."

"You're welcome." She dug in her laptop bag and pulled out another protein bar. "Last one. Seriously, do I need to split this with you or will we be eating soon?"

"If I know my sister, she has food for us."

"Food, food? Not just ingredient-type food."

Headlights pulling around the building had him reaching for his weapon instead of answering that Gillie never had ingredients. "It's okay. That's Gillie. Take everything with you. We won't be back."

She grabbed her heels, stuffing them in the side pocket of her laptop bag.

"Shoot, Jack." His sister punched his arm lightly. "You said Megan needed dry clothes, but he failed to mention she was freezing. Can you hang on ten more minutes until we get back to my place?"

"Oh, sure. I'm all numb now. As long as you have some food. Even a real sugary cereal will do."

"I've got both. Don't worry."

While he transferred everything, both women climbed into the smaller and older truck his sister had borrowed from the ranch. He wasn't certain it was licensed for the road, but it ran.

Bouncing down the road in a vehicle with basically no shocks, he once again listened to Megan and Gillie talk as if they'd known each other more than two days and were best friends.

Megan basically filled his sister in on all the details, including their game of strip Battleship. He covered his face with his hand and looked out the window. The rain had passed to the north, where he could still see the lightning. The direction they were headed had clear skies and stars.

"Isn't that right, Jack?"

"Huh?"

"I said," his sister emphasized, "you were looking forward to seeing your high-school teammates again. And that I hoped this was all wrapped up before the game Friday. Mrs. Dennis was *so* not happy when you didn't show for the meeting."

"I thought it was homecoming."

"It's a special gathering, since the football team's headed to state again."

"The last time they went, Jack was the quarterback."

"Oh! I get it now. That's the game Carl Ray back at the diner was talking about. The one they rerun on television because of a last-minute super throw or something like that," Megan said.

"So," his sister began with teasing in her voice, "do I need to make up the couch or are you good with sharing the spare bedroom?"

"We won't be here that long." He spoke louder than Megan's affirmative answer that one bed would be spectacular.

"When's the last time you slept, Jack? Thursday?" his sister asked. "Maybe you should catch a couple of hours while I look after Megan."

"Honestly, Megan doesn't need looking after," Megan answered, sounding annoyed.

"You're right. My apologies. After the couple of days you've had, I'm sure you can," his sister amended.

Come to think about it, he hadn't slept since Thursday. Not really. Not for more than twenty-minute stretches. Tonight could be different. "Maybe I could manage a couple of hours. That is, if Megan doesn't mind."

"You know I don't. I'll be fine." She squeezed his hand.

So was the gesture just a gesture? Was it thanks for asking her opinion? Or was it the next step in something he was starting to hope could develop into more?

Gillie turned the old truck onto the road where her house was located. It had belonged to his uncle's family eons ago, before his death. Before his father had bought them out to ensure that the property stayed in the family. Jack's body was powering down, accepting permission to sleep.

They cornered the last turn to the house, and

Gillie skidded to a stop. The house was lit with flashing red, white and blue lights. At least three police cars and two black SUVs were parked with their headlights trained on the front door. Another official vehicle pulled across the drive behind them.

They were boxed in.

Megan squeezed his hand, then laced her fingers with his. "I guess this means no sugar flakes."

Chapter Sixteen

"Before you say anything stupid, I did *not* call Dad," Gillie said, banging her hand on the steering wheel. "It must have been Oscar."

"It looks like officers are approaching the truck and I think they have their weapons drawn." Megan's hand was still holding on to Jack's. She covered her eyes with her free hand before the flashing lights made her tired brain seize.

"Gillie, get out. Raise your hands, call out to Dad and then walk toward him. And be careful. No sudden movements. You know the drill."

"Sure. You aren't going to do anything stupid, like try to leave in this broken-down thing. Are you?" his sister asked.

"No. I have to make a phone call and we'll be right behind you."

Jack squeezed Megan's hand and let go, putting his right hand on the dash and removing his phone with his left. As it powered up, it began dinging with notification after notification.

"Do you want mine?" she asked.

"No, but put your left hand on the dash so they can see it. We don't want them to get trigger-happy." His eyes locked with hers, giving her courage.

Strange how that worked.

"How come I'm more afraid now than when those guys were shooting at us? Or when I was alone with that man who didn't think I could swing a poker?"

"I get it. But nothing's going to happen. These are the good guys and don't forget...my dad's a senator. Use your right hand and play the last message from Wade."

"Get out of the car!" a man said with a bullhorn.

The voice message played. "Jack, I get why you aren't calling or checking in. Saw the news. Nothing is right about this gig. Not the girl, the crew, the reason. Supposed to be returning a favor for rescuing your hide—yeah, I owe you another explanation about that. I'm on the trail of the people behind your ambush in Austin. Sorry about this, partner. Contact border-style."

"What does that mean? He didn't mention Therese. Or me. I'm far from being a girl."

"These details are for if the police listen to the message. We had a drop when I was undercover. There's a place in Dallas that matches up. Megan—"

She turned the phone off, dropped it in her laptop bag and turned her face toward his. "So what's the plan? Are we honest with them and tell them everything?"

"Of course, but wait on a lawyer. Cops can be tricky." Jack winked and turned his shoulders in the first movement to get out of the car.

"Ranger MacKinnon, put your hands out the window. Now!" said the bullhorn man.

He turned the window crank. "I'm getting out, and I'm unarmed."

"Tell them I begged for your help. It might save your job."

Jack quickly turned and took her face between his hands. He brought his lips to hers, a second kiss just as passionate as the first. Even if the situation this time was desperate, the kiss was beautiful and comforting. Instead of being filled by the hope of what questions might come, it was filled with the dread that they knew the answer.

The men surrounding the truck finished their advance. Jack raised his hands. "I'm not lying, Megan. Neither should you. And don't forget, we have some unfinished...um... Battleship business."

He purposely accentuated his dimples.

"I knew you could use those at your will." She

would have responded with more if she hadn't been dragged by her borrowed flannel shirt out the other side of the truck.

The next minutes were a long blur. At least Gillie was free. Jack was handcuffed and facing a man who paced back and forth on the porch. She sat in one of the state troopers' cars, hands behind her back, totally uncomfortable on the plastic seat, afraid to move. She was paralyzed. First because she hated not knowing what would happen and secondly the ick factor. Sitting on a seat that could be hosed out made her wonder what had been there before her.

Two cars remained, and both officers were standing out of earshot of the porch conversation. Her window was cracked and she could finally hear a little of what was going on.

"I *am* your father, and you *will* listen to me," said the man pacing. Well, that settled who he was.

Jack looked nothing like him, with the exception of the dimples in their chins. The older man was several inches shorter, graying at the temples and wearing a suit. But he exuded authority—especially over Gillie and her brother.

"Take those cuffs off him and bring in the girl," he directed.

"We need to take Miss Harper in for questioning, Mayor MacKinnon."

"Officer Scranton, I'm the one who brought you here. Don't you think I know that you'll be taking her back to Austin? But first, I'd like to speak to her and my son. And remember, you're in my town. I could lock them up here and you could just wait your turn. Or I can insist that you go through proper channels and file all the appropriate paperwork required to transfer from my city to yours. Do you want that?"

"Bring Miss Harper inside and stay posted at the doors." Bullhorn man had also succumbed to the powerful Mr. MacKinnon.

Thing was, she was used to a man like Jack Sr. She'd wrapped someone just like him around her pinkie finger all her life. He wouldn't like weak or tired. He'd appreciate someone honest and straightforward. But would it do her any good to try?

Jack stood at attention once inside the small living room. It was a position that Megan was extremely familiar with as a child of a military officer. He also seemed to be avoiding eye contact with Megan. Was he blaming himself? Or attempting not to draw attention to her?

Gillie plopped on the couch and toed off her boots. Her head dropped to the top of the cushion, and she let out a long sigh but kept staring at the ceiling.

"What in the hell are you thinking?" Jack Sr. began—or should she think of him as Senator?

"Can you stop the bluster now, Dad? Everyone's out of earshot." Gillie grabbed a pillow and hugged it to her body, subconsciously getting an additional layer of protection. "I know you're happy they're both safe."

Jack Sr. took a dining-room chair, flipped it around and invited Megan to sit. It was on the tip of her tongue to refuse, but Gillie caught her eye and ever so slightly suggested a no with her chin. Then she looked toward her brother.

"Thank you, sir," Megan said, trusting the siblings to handle the person they'd grown up with.

He looked at her with a surprised expression that Jack and Gillie both had in their repertoire. *This should be fun.*

Well, it would be if she weren't in handcuffs.

"Come on, Dad," Gillie whined again.

It was an act. An overexaggeration for some reason. And then Megan witnessed the magic of being daddy's little girl.

"I'll get the patrolman to unlock—"

"No need." Gillie popped up and removed a small key from a box on a lower cabinet shelf. "Oh, Dad. Don't get any ideas. Little Jack gave me this years ago in case something happened."

Jack Sr. cleared his throat.

"Nothing like that. I was undercover. I didn't

know if I'd be any good at it, so I took precautions if someone linked me back to the ranch. There's one in your house. Mom knows where."

Jack Sr. waved him off. "We should get to the matter at hand before the men outside gather their courage. How can I help clear up this mess, son?"

Megan was confused. Even more so when Gillie unlocked her handcuffs, put a finger to her lips and sat again.

"Oscar came to the house?" Jack asked.

"I think he was on his way to the house before Gillie pulled off the property," his dad said.

"And your detail got wind of everything?" Gillie asked. "Why didn't you call me?"

"Obvious political reasons, sweetheart. This was the best I could do after the fact. If you'd come to me—"

"We can discuss how you help me and Gillie at another time." Jack finally moved, scratching his chin and thinking.

She'd observed him so many times in the past couple of days that she was familiar with his process. This was normally the time that she interjected, but she'd take the advice handed to her minutes ago and stay quiet.

Well, there was one suggestion. "If I may?"

Both Jacks and Gillie snapped their heads around to look at her. She waited for permission.

That was strange and not something she wanted to become a habit. Jack raised a questioning eyebrow.

"If I could use my laptop to check information about the case and check my messages."

"Absolutely not!"

"Dad," the siblings said together.

"It's actually a good idea," Jack defended. "Didn't you mention that you've got a portable external hard drive with you?"

"Is that even legal?" his dad asked.

"I was on a case in Dallas and needed access to my files. There shouldn't have been anything sensitive in what I took with me."

"Then I don't see the point."

"It might help us. I thought you wanted us out of your hair."

"I didn't say that." He turned to Gillie. "Did I say anything like that?"

Gillie slapped the sofa cushion, pushing herself to her feet. "I'll have Scranton get the bag. And I'm telling Mom that neither one of you gets access to the Cowboys game on Thanksgiving Day until you talk all this mess out."

"That's not necessary."

Gillie smiled at her brother and father. "Oh, yeah, it definitely is."

Officer Scranton reluctantly opened the laptop bag, knowing that it broke so many rules they wouldn't fit on one page. But apparently, he'd served on several of the same cases as Jack. He sighed and said he'd video the entire thing, which seemed to satisfy everyone.

Megan opened the secured laptop and hard drive, not only allowing Scranton to use his phone to record her passwords, but also writing them down along with the files she was accessing.

"This is taking longer than I'd hoped," Jack Sr. stated on one of his passes around the dining-room table. "Are you sure you need to write it all down?"

"I don't want anything we find to be thrown out in court. We're risking a lot doing this here." Megan wrote another file name down. "We've been tossing around ideas for two days. Honestly, this might be the last copy of some of these files."

"Young lady, I have no idea what you're searching for. Nor do I want to know. Don't think that you have anything to do with receiving help from me. I'm here solely to clear my son's name."

"You're on tape, Dad," Gillie reminded him while Jack Jr. first rolled then covered his eyes.

"Yes, I know. I'm still uncertain how this family even became involved in this mess."

"One word… Wade," Gillie said, summing up the explanation.

"You've got to be kidding."

Megan tried to ignore the conversation as she searched the files. She couldn't wait to meet

Wade. She owed him a great deal. The man who was responsible for bringing Jack into her life. Who knew what might have happened if he hadn't convinced his partner to meet her at the airport?

"These are the files associated with Harry Knight." She turned the laptop to where they could all look at them. "I'm uncertain why anyone would want to kill him over his notary signature. It's not like his office isn't responsible for hundreds of these a day."

"Didn't you mention that he personally signed these and that was the only strange thing?" Jack asked.

"Yes, but even then—"

"Why is that strange?" Gillie and Scranton asked.

"Because he's the head of the office," Megan began. "Not someone at the front desk."

"An elected official would oversee things, direct," Jack Sr. finished. "He goes to meetings. He doesn't pull the notary stamp out and verify signatures for just anyone. Let me see those."

"Every property ending with a fire has his personal signature."

Jack Sr. took a seat next to Megan and scrolled through the scanned copies of documents. "This has to be what started everything. Miss Harper, I think you're being framed. And I think I can help you connect some dots."

Chapter Seventeen

"Good old-fashioned insurance fraud with a twenty-first-century twist," his father explained to the state attorney general. "I agree. Knight wasn't the random victim everyone thought. Yes. Yes, that's my son's company. I'll pass your instructions along. Thank you."

The officers waited patiently on the front porch. Gillie had shut herself behind her bedroom door. Megan sat on the couch beside him—actually, handcuffed to him. There was only so far the officers would trust Jack Sr., even if he was a newly elected state senator.

Until they were ordered otherwise, technically Jack and Megan were still wanted for questioning in Austin and Dallas. The officers didn't know they had nowhere to go. After his dad cleared the air, he would take Megan to headquarters for protection.

"He's bringing in the Rangers to handle the

City of Dallas investigation," his father explained. "You'll be briefed when you arrive in Dallas."

"Really? Just one phone call." Megan leaned closer. "Your dad got everything taken care of with one phone call."

"Yep." He wasn't resentful, but he didn't exactly have to be glad about it. Yet. Fixing this problem was out of his hands. It always had been.

"You have to admit the fraud was very hard to pick up on. Different buyers of buildings that couldn't legally be sold. Shouldn't have been sold because they're in probate or the heirs can't be found."

"All abandoned buildings lost to fire. It might have taken years to come to the attention of my department." Megan looked like she was enjoying the brainstorming session.

"And yet someone sent you to check it out. You're not sure who or why. And they didn't give you a heads-up about what to look for."

"I see your point. I can admit that I'm being framed."

"You have an enemy out there. That's certain," Jack Sr. said, leaning back in the chair.

"An enemy that loves fire," Jack pointed out.

"That should be easy to narrow down."

"Only if you had a list to begin with," Megan admitted.

"Don't you? Have a list, I mean." Jack thought

it would be pretty easy from this point. "You work for the state fire marshal. How hard can it be to get a list of arsons matching the fire particulars?"

"That's just it. All the fires are different. Arsonists normally stick to one type of device. Psychopaths definitely do and want to watch. Those files represented seven completely different buildings. Seven locations. Seven types of fuel that all look accidental. Seven different times of day."

"I get it. That's the reason authorities didn't make the connection." He wrapped his handcuffed hand over hers and released it just as quickly. The last thing he needed was his dad racing to the conclusion that he was involved with Megan.

He might want to be, but he wasn't.

Yet.

That was a big *yet*.

"Can you call Scranton inside, son?" His dad shut the laptop and leaned back in his chair.

Jack locked his fingers around Megan's wrist and pulled her to her feet as he stood. They worked together without words and waved the officer inside.

"The attorney general needs to know your supervisor's number. He'll make the official call to you. I don't want anyone accusing us of letting Little Jack go because of my new status."

Scranton nodded and took himself back outside.

"What happens now?" Megan asked.

"Well, you can let yourself out of those handcuffs, for one." His dad tossed him the key he'd given Gillie months ago. "Then you can tell me more about yourself."

"Dad, I appreciate—"

"Let me stop you right there, son. You don't have a vehicle, you look like you're exhausted and you're probably hungry. We can go back up to the main house, have some dinner and you two can get a good night's sleep. All this will be waiting on you in the morning."

What ulterior motive could his father have? As nice as the man was…there was always an ulterior motive.

"Sounds wonderful. I'm dying for a hot bath after the dousing in the creek this morning. I think my toes are still blue."

"Then it's settled. Let me check on Scranton." His father left, closing the door gently behind him.

"Are they gone?" Gillie asked from the doorway leading to the bedrooms.

"Yes. But Dad's up to something. Unless you want to have dinner up at the house, you should stay in your room."

She waved him off and tossed some clothes at Megan. "Dad's always up to something. You're older than me. You should know that by now."

He was and he did.

The conversation quickly turned to clothes and

houses being blown to bits and back to shoes. Jack stood at the window, watching his father in his political stance—shaking hands and gripping the other man's shoulder.

He shouldn't care that his father would choose to remind him about the help he'd given. It was the same with everything that Little Jack MacKinnon took on. None of that really worried him. What did was fending off the obvious argument that would be coming to a head tonight if they had dinner with his parents.

Life-altering decisions were always discussed at dinner. It didn't matter that Megan would be there. Nope. His dad would push forward on his position that only his son was qualified to follow in his footsteps.

Jack dropped his head to the thick windowpane as the officers got into the two remaining patrol cars and pulled away. His dad waved at him and got into his black SUV. He hadn't bothered to verify that Jack actually saw the gesture. It didn't matter, since one of his men would have come to knock on the door.

"He looks very accustomed to that sort of life," Gillie said over his shoulder, offering a hug. Then she opened the door for her guests to leave. "The guards only showed up yesterday after I told him they'd blown up your house. Night, guys."

"You aren't coming to dinner?" Megan asked.

"That's all you, big brother. Good luck." She shook her head and smiled at him. "I have leftovers from yesterday's meeting."

MEGAN HAD AN image of what she thought a senator's home would be like. Okay, money. She'd imagined money. The house was nice, simple, updated but old. It turned out that the stairs creaked and the bathroom door stuck. And Jack's mom had to quickly defrost chicken for dinner.

Defrosting of another kind was on Megan's mind as she luxuriated in the steel claw-foot tub and used every bit of the hot water.

"You ready to eat?" Jack's voice was at the door just as the bathwater began to cool.

"I'll be right there, Little Jack."

"There's no need to get nasty. You got your bath." His footsteps disappeared down the staircase.

True. She'd gotten her bath and was clean. Mrs. MacKinnon had set out flannel pajamas and thick woolen socks. She'd mentioned that Gillie had given her a heads-up about Megan's frozen toes.

As she stepped off the last stair, she turned to find parents and son in a deep whispered discussion.

"I hope I'm not interrupting."

"I was just telling Mom and Dad that we probably shouldn't discuss the case." Jack pulled out her chair at the beautifully set dining table. "Or other subjects that might get heated."

"Oh, don't stop because of me."

Lena MacKinnon burst out laughing. "Little Jack said we'd like you."

Everyone sat, and dishes went around. Simple yet delicious. It felt like she was back at her mother's table.

"I've got to say, Lena, that I'm impressed. This is wonderful. My manners insist that I apologize for putting you out like this, but your chicken is amazing."

"I'm so glad you like it. I can give you the recipe if you'd like it."

"Megan doesn't cook," Jack said before she could finish her bite and answer for herself.

"I'd love the recipe. Thanks." She turned to Jack, who sat next to her, and said, "I can read, silly."

"You just currently don't have a kitchen." Jack shoved another bite of the chicken into his mouth.

True. It didn't get past her that he was in a crisp white button-down shirt and looking all cowboy handsome with a freshly shaved face and slicked-back wet hair.

She should tone down her banter and act like her mother's child. Polite. Well mannered. Businesslike. She could do that if she tried. But Jack was just so darn easy to tease.

The tension between him and his father was a forbidden conversation. She knew that and had an idea of what it concerned. So most of the conversation was about the upcoming homecoming festivities.

"The kids are decorating windows tomorrow. Will you be back in time to supervise, Little Jack?" Lena asked.

"Afraid not. I need to head to Dallas after I drop Megan off at headquarters."

"What's so important in Dallas?" Jack Sr. said, tightening the tension even more. "I simply don't understand your apathetic attitude toward life. You have a commitment to Liberty Hill this week."

"I also have a commitment to my partner, who's missing."

"You're certain? I thought you needed to make contact." Why was adrenaline soaring through her veins? She was ready to forgo dinner cleanup, additional teasing and, most important, sleep. They should be on the road, tracking down Wade.

"I've made some calls. No one's seen him since Thursday."

"Wade Hamilton is not your responsibility."

"We should change the subject, Jack. He asked us not to talk about this tonight." Lena patted her husband's arm as he put down his fork.

"My apologies, Miss Harper. There never seems to be a right time for this conversation." Jack Sr.

stood and dropped his napkin in his chair, giving a stern look at his son.

"That's because it's the wrong conversation. I chose a different life, Dad. I'm over thirty. Successful. And a part of an elite law-enforcement agency that lots of good men never break into. Don't bother getting up. I'm asleep on my feet and ready to turn in."

"I think I'll head up, too," Megan said while chewing the last bite of chicken. "Thank you so much. Don't hate me for not cleaning up."

Jack was already halfway up the stairs, but he waited for her. Both his parents assured her helping with the dishes wasn't necessary and wished her good-night. He'd lost it. Not badly, but she knew he'd done exactly what he didn't want to do.

When she caught up with him, he pointed to her room in the middle of the hall next to the bath. "I'm at the end." He pointed a little farther.

"Want to talk about it?"

"We already have." They stopped at her open door.

"Are you really worried about your partner?" she whispered.

He nodded and realized Wade wasn't just an excuse to get away from his father. "Somebody in Company B should have heard from him. He might be a seat-of-his-pants sort of guy, but he knows what happens when a ranger goes missing."

All hell broke loose for sure.

"I'm going with you," Megan said as quietly as before.

"No. You're not."

Megan copied the way he was standing and mimicked what he thought had been a look of determination. "Putting your hands on your hips isn't going to get your way. I think if I went back downstairs, I could convince both your mom and dad that my expertise is needed in Dallas. I can answer questions there."

He gently shoved her through the door and closed it behind him.

"Why do you want to go with me? You need to be in protective custody. Somebody's trying to kill you." Like she didn't know that already.

She quickly slid her arms across his chest and around his neck. "I am in protective custody."

He grabbed her wrists, ready to pull her hands away, but didn't really want to. "I shouldn't be here. This is my parents' house."

"You're right." She tugged his ear to her mouth, scraping her teeth along its ridge. "I can't risk that you're a screamer."

That's it.

Jack wrapped his arms tightly around her, leaving no space between his shirt and her borrowed pajamas. He stretched her body until her mouth was even with his. Then he started kissing the soft area where her neck and shoulder connected.

Her breath quickened. So did his.

She tried to break free from his mouth and return the intimacy. He kept his mouth against her skin.

She wiggled. He pulled her body in tighter.

She turned her face to his. He kissed her like he'd never kissed anyone before. And he kissed her again. And then again.

She tried to back up. He planted his feet firmly apart.

"Not here. I'm not letting our first time together be in a room above my parents." He kissed her long and hard, stretching the last moments, tasting more than just the spices from dinner. He tasted what he knew was her unique flavor.

"I get it." She kissed him again. "The psychological damage it might do to you is too great to think about."

"You are definitely a tease," he said between more kisses.

"Jack," his father said with a soft knock on the door.

Even though he hadn't planned to go any further than kissing Megan, having his dad interrupt and send him to his childhood bedroom wasn't pleasant. That psychological damage might happen anyway.

"Yes?" Jack answered when he could breathe normally.

"The men will be heading to Austin first thing in the morning. I told them to expect Megan. That'll save you some time."

Megan shook her head, mouthing "no."

"Good night, son."

Jack stepped away from Megan and pulled the door open.

"I appreciate the time-saver, but I'll drop Megan off in the morning. I gave my word to keep her safe."

His father turned, mumbling another good-night as he headed downstairs.

Jack leaned against the doorjamb, amazed that his mind had changed so quickly about keeping her with him. "He's right. You should go back with the armed escort. You'd be safer and…yeah, definitely safer."

"What's the fun in that?" She winked and closed the door.

Chapter Eighteen

The phone rang, and Alvie Balsawood swiped the reject button. Even if he'd been prepared to deal with the question he was certain would be asked, he was in the security line at the airport. Summoned to Dallas by his partners, he needed to deal with the problem Megan Harper had created.

The men on loan from the money side of the partnership had barely cleared the vehicles before the Wimberley police had arrived. They'd been full of one excuse after another and whined about injuries. If he'd been in the same room, he might have committed murder himself.

As it was, he'd barely contained his rage and limited it to turning the stereo on high and yelling under its noise. His neighbors banged on the walls, but nothing else happened.

He'd warned his partners that meeting in person wasn't a good idea. In fact, it was a terrible idea. He hadn't secured all the potential copies of the files, and they hadn't secured Megan or either of the men sent to keep her from harm's way.

Through with security, he stood in line for a coffee and breakfast sandwich. He wasn't going to starve just because he was on a flight. The phone rang again. He glanced at the caller ID and swiped Reject…again.

He searched the crowd, wondering if any suspicious men were around to drug him like they had done to Megan. They probably did have someone watching to verify he got on the plane. But what they didn't know was that he'd already transferred all the money to an offshore account. He wasn't heading to Dallas for the big explanation meeting on a plastic sheet that could be used to dispose of his corpse.

No, sir, there'd be no last-minute murder of Alvie Balsawood. He was too smart. This whole scam had been his idea. Dallas had worldwide connecting flights, and he intended to use one.

He was escaping while he still could before he was caught and couldn't name his partners for a deal. Yes, he could describe Therese, the one person he'd been face-to-face with. Anyone could tell she wasn't the money or decision maker.

That left Alvie with nothing. No bargaining chips and totally expendable to the money person. As badly as he wanted Megan to fall from grace or be executed on her knees, he had a greater desire to live the rest of his days on a beach.

"DOES HE THINK he can take my money and just fly away?" Rushdan Reval shoved his finger into his wide-open mouth to pick a last bite of food from his teeth.

Undercover for almost eight months, Therese Ortis watched. The overfed, overindulged, totally spoiled twentysomething Rushdan dragged the fingernail along his desk. She closed her eyes while he used the same finger for a toothpick again. The habit was disgusting. Made more so because she wasn't allowed to do anything accept watch while it took place.

It was a part of his thought process. If she looked away, he'd think she wasn't listening and only bring her closer.

So she waited, watching the sun push upward over Dallas, reflecting off the glass high-rises. Rushdan had moved to the fifth floor of his new and unfinished building on the south side. It was rare to be called to her employer's office this early. She normally oversaw his night interests.

"The plan is solid, with one glitch," he finally continued, "whoever gave the warning to Wade Hamilton. Get rid of that problem and the three subsequent errors are easily eliminated. Then we're back in business."

He dropped his heavy body into a chair near the windows, his back to her. Another indicator that he really didn't expect her to answer. She might stand here for a half hour without uttering a word, then be dismissed.

It might be because she didn't complain that he spoke so freely to her. She didn't mind. Her real job was to listen and send the information back to her true employer.

"But who is the traitor, do you think? Not Balsawood, obviously."

Therese was careful to keep her expressions minimal. She didn't want to react to his conclusions—just in case he might actually suspect her.

Since she *was* the person who brought the authorities into the mix. She'd done it against her handler's recommendation. She'd even risked her cover by sending the information to her supervisor. But when Megan had been sent to investigate, the opportunity to bring in a separate agency seemed the logical choice.

Right up until Rushdan was notified by that creepy state insurance guy who'd come up with the insurance-fraud scheme. A scheme that had absolutely nothing to do with why she'd gone undercover with Rushdan's organization, which was the reason her superiors didn't want her to risk the work they'd done to find out where the real money came from.

"Do you have any theories, Therese?"

"Pardon?" she said softly.

She glanced slightly behind her at the two men standing guard on either side of the door. Neither had a weapon in hand and neither seemed to have itchy fingers. That might be a good sign.

"I know that you're friends with Megan Harper, the stupid almost cop that's ruining my sweet insurance profit."

"I don't understand, Rushdy," she answered with her best innocent attitude. "I want to help, but can you remind me which Megan we're talking about? Is she the one in the kitchen or out front? And oh, I think one just works Tuesday through Thursday on account of college classes. What did this chica do?"

Rushdan flicked a finger. "Bring him in."

One guard opened the door. The other waved. Two additional men she'd seen around the nightclub dragged a man between them into the middle of the room.

"I'm sorry you have to witness this, honey, but I need some answers."

One of the guys kicked the captive's ribs. He moaned and covered his middle, protecting himself from another blow.

"Damn, you can stop anytime now."

Wade Hamilton. It was the only man it could

be if it involved the insurance fraud. She knew they'd been tracking him. And she knew his voice.

Startled could no longer be a part of her vocabulary or reactions. Training had helped, but after eight months of being around beaten men and abused women every day, she'd become numb—or self-preservation had kicked in.

"Do you know this man, Therese?"

She hoped and prayed that Wade could keep his own surprise under control. He had no idea who she was or what she did.

"Is this Megan? No wonder I was confused, Rushdy. I assumed it was a girl, but you can never tell nowadays." She hid a short laugh behind her hand. "Sorry. No. I don't think I've seen this guy. Was he a problem at one of the clubs?"

"This is a different problem. You sure you don't recognize him?"

"He might have come by, but he ain't no regular." She bent down to make eye contact, hoping Wade could keep it together. Their eyes locked. Hers with what she had practiced as confusion and his full of defiance. "No. He seems a little old for my places."

"Probably. You'll let me know if anyone comes asking questions about him."

"Sure thing. Is there anything else?"

"You're good, Therese. I'll check in this afternoon for my usual."

"I'll tell the chef."

Therese had to step over Wade's body on her way out of the room. Her mouth and throat were so dry she swung by the break room down the hall for a bottle of water. There were all sorts of illegal snacks in the refrigerator. She was careful to check the seals and make sure the bottle didn't leak prior to drinking.

Slipping young women drugs was commonplace here. And yet another illegal activity her bosses weren't concerned with. When she took these men down...there would be so much satisfaction.

Once in the stairwell, she was unsure how she'd managed to stay on her heels. It was the first time in months that she'd felt she might not make it out alive.

All for a woman she'd barely known two years ago but had changed her life with a simple comment of going after what she wanted. Therese had been recruited for special training soon after.

Everything would be on schedule if she'd obeyed her supervisors, should have listened to her handler, should have kept her nose out of this scam and stuck with her real objective—finding Rushdan's funds and the men writing his programming.

Hell, why not go a step further? She paused on the stairs while she thought everything through.

They'd eventually lock Wade up on the first floor. She could get in that room—it was just a matter of avoiding cameras and not being seen. A hat and a pair of overalls would help with that.

Everything was already at risk. Megan, Wade Hamilton...even her own life. Why not jeopardize eight months of undercover work?

Chapter Nineteen

"One call?" Looking frustrated, Megan pushed her fingers through her hair, gathered it together at the base of her neck and fluffed it out again. "I'm really amazed that your dad made one call and cleared me so I could come with you today. And that he woke the state attorney general up from a nap."

They'd been on the road for four hours, but Megan had only been awake the last fifteen or twenty minutes. He missed the banter when she was asleep, but the conversation about his dad could wait.

"Tell me why we didn't contact your father when you had me handcuffed to your end table two days ago?"

Or maybe not.

"You know why. At that time you were headed to the Rangers."

"I think it has something to do with you not wanting to talk to your father."

"Tread lightly."

Jack was about to state that they'd already been over those details, but something stopped him. That involuntary prevention stemmed from a place buried deep in his head that had something to do with relationships. Or the need for sleep. He'd had little of either recently.

Megan hadn't asked a real question. She was making a point, still believing it was a matter of pride that had kept him away from his father.

"You're wrong."

"About…?" she asked.

"It isn't pride like you're thinking. We had limited choices at the time. We didn't know if the SUV guys would follow from the diner or if they'd hurt my family. We didn't have any idea they had the resources that they did. Heading south actually gave us a lot of information about our opponents."

"That's true. Waiting also got us frozen. Oh, wait—that was just me. Plus a wrecked truck—totally you—and almost killed. Okay, that was the both of us. Other than that, we're good."

Exchanging veiled barbs with Megan was new territory. She was someone he wanted to pursue a relationship with. He'd been the first—okay, the second—to admit that his father had gotten them free and saved a lot of hassle, headlines and reprimands at Company B.

Now he and Megan were free to make calls and investigate without avoiding the police. But he wouldn't admit to anyone that avoiding everyone for two days had been the wrong decision. It had also given them time to get to know each other.

"Dammit, for once in my life, I'd prefer a woman who can just tell me what she means. You know?" He must really be more tired than he'd admitted to anyone or even himself. He hadn't meant to lead with that blunt statement.

Megan laughed. "I have never been accused—" she laughed harder "—of being coy or not speaking my mind."

"Sorry," he mumbled, knowing he really was.

"For what? For speaking yours? Do you really think I'd talk to you freely and not expect the same from you?"

"Honestly, I don't know what to think about. I've never met anyone like you. And don't expect that I will again."

And he hadn't. Toni was the only woman he'd taken on a fourth date, and he'd eventually asked her to marry him. He could acknowledge that Wade had more experience when it came to dating. But the possibility of dropping Megan off and never seeing her again… His mind kept shouting that he couldn't let that happen.

"Wait just a second, Little Jack. That sounds dangerously close to attraction."

"You're a smart woman, Megan. I don't believe you ever thought otherwise."

"Okay, kidding aside. You're a cool guy. When all this is done, I could see us going on a date or two. The long-distance commute thing might present a problem. But we have to find your partner and the people behind this madness before we think about that."

"Agreed." On everything except the one or two dates. He had every intention of taking her on a fourth. Then a fifth.

Damn, he was seriously attracted to Megan.

"Does it worry you that your partner hasn't checked in since that message yesterday?"

"No. Yes, but he said 'border-style,' which means no communication until I check the drop."

"I'm completely changing the subject, but I still can't get over how quickly your dad found the link to all those fires."

"A link, yes, but we still don't know who's behind everything or why your friend Therese warned you."

"Acquaintance. We were in the San Antonio PD academy together. I think we had drinks and one profound conversation about going for what we wanted. She resigned soon after. I have no idea how she'd know my life was in danger."

"Or how she rescued me from the border. As far as connecting the dots of the fires goes, I'm sure you would have. No one gave you a chance." Thinking about his dad's feat, it was sort of amazing that he'd put everything together so quickly.

"Sure. Back in my quiet office, where you wanted me to be today. Why didn't you want me to investigate the rest of this case with you? Tired of me?"

"I'm escorting you to the Dallas PD so you can give a statement, Megan. That's all. Dropping you off. Not taking you with me to meet Wade."

"Or find him if he's in trouble. I understood and agreed that was the only option, Little Jack. But I don't have to like it."

"You're making that very clear." *Little Jack.* Man, he hated that nickname. "Actually, my dad was a hell of a cop. Little towns like Liberty Hill might not have a lot of crime, but being the chief of police, he had more to do than just handing out citations or—"

"Or directing the homecoming parade?"

"Yes."

"Can I be honest?"

"Have you been anything else?" he asked, truly curious.

"I guess I haven't. I sat handcuffed in that patrol car thinking I was going to dislike your father. After what you told me, it sounded like he deliberately ruined your operation for his own political gain. You know, he sounded like a politician."

"Don't let the niceness and competence fool you. He has a very hands-on campaign. He approved the TV ad about me becoming a ranger. And he's a good enough cop to know *why* I wasn't available for his spotlights."

"You're much calmer than I would be."

"I've had some time off to think about it." He took the last sip of his coffee. "Enough time for Wade to get me into another mess. No offense."

"It's okay. I totally get it. None of this was your choice."

"I wouldn't say that. I seem to recall choosing the diner, which is the first place they caught up to us. Then I chose where we stayed for two nights, and they caught up with us again. And last night, since it was my family, you could probably assume that was my choice, too."

"Stop. I'm laughing so hard you're going to be forced to make a pit stop."

It was good to hear laughter about everything. She laughed so hard she practically snorted, making her laugh harder. *Whoa, man.* He was falling too hard, too fast, and knew almost nothing about this woman.

"So why, after living all over the world, did you decide to live in Texas?" he asked. If he was falling, he could get the ball rolling to become better acquainted.

"Why not? Don't Texans believe this is the best place on the planet?"

"Texans might, but what about you?"

"Honestly, it was one of the last places Dad was stationed, and I actually had a few friends here. Mom and Dad went back to England when I started college. I received my degree and immediately went into the San Antonio Police Academy and began a life here. There's nothing much to it."

"School and field of studies? You're skipping the details." His phone began buzzing and he caught the number. *Major Clements.* "My company commander. I need to take this. Looks like you're going to get that pit stop."

He let the phone go to voice mail while he pulled over at a convenience store. Even though it was an unscheduled stop, he checked the place for the SUV men and woman.

"Lock the door and knock before you come out. I'll be two steps away."

MEGAN WOULD HAVE laughed off Jack's precautions, but he'd been pretty accurate about safety.

The questions didn't bother her. She understood that she'd met his entire family and he knew little to nothing about hers. She'd rather be going through the points of the case and was antsy to follow the adventure through to the end. She normally didn't get to do that.

Okay, so she'd done it once in a much smaller, local venue. But this was different. Catching a murderer seemed more important than a kid with kerosene and a lighter.

A glance at herself in the mirror made her wonder why Jack was interested at all. Everything she had was borrowed and would continue to be. It hadn't really sunk in just how much she'd lost.

These people had blown up her house, for crying out loud. Everything except a few mementos could be replaced. She knew that. But they were still *her* things. And each time she thought about it, she felt guilty because two people had died.

Jack knocked again, and she tucked herself close to his side as they left the convenience store.

"I told you before, it's okay to mourn your loss," he said once they were inside the car.

"How did you know I was thinking about my house?"

"For one thing, you're not talking about me or my dad." He shrugged. "You get a far-off kind of look where you don't focus on anything. Only happened a couple of times. Mostly you don't drift. You're aware of your surroundings all the time."

"How do you…? You barely know me."

"Yeah, sometimes I amaze myself." He caught

her hand in his. "You worried about the insurance paying up? Or was something special there?"

"My parents never owned a house. Don't get me wrong—we had plenty of homes all over the world. But we were never in a place long enough for them to actually own it."

"So it was a first. I get it."

"I doubt you do. Your mother mentioned your ranch has been in your family for three generations."

"Yeah, one man's dream…another man's nightmare. The main reason my father wants me to follow in his footsteps is to take over the ranch. Tradition." He shrugged as he had so often throughout the weekend. She was beginning to think that he wasn't as casual about things as he let everyone believe.

"And here I thought that not having any traditions was a problem. I guess you're right. Hmm… that grass-is-always-greener thing may be true."

His phone rang. He let go of her hand to answer and steer the borrowed SUV. She immediately missed his warmth and reassurance.

How long had it been since she'd felt reassured by just being with someone? Maybe since her parents had moved—at least on this comfort scale. She attempted not to listen, which was quite impossible in a vehicle.

There were a lot of *yes, sir*s and *no, sir*s and

*right away, sir*s. It ended with a "straight to their office. I understand." The way that Jack dropped his phone in the cup holder didn't bode well that it had been a casual call.

"Should I ask?"

"No need. I've been instructed to take you directly to the Dallas PD, then proceed directly to Company B headquarters."

"Do not pass Go. Do not collect two hundred dollars."

"That's about right."

"Are you in big trouble for helping me? You aren't going to lose your job or anything, are you?"

"Not according to Dad. My commander made it clear he didn't like a future senator in his job assignments. So it might depend on the state of my partner."

"Aren't you going to your drop point? We could go there instead of taking me to the police." She paused, letting him laugh and rub his chin. "Why are you laughing? Isn't that what you called it?"

"I was going there right after dropping you off."

"So you are a little rebellious."

"I call it being practical."

"Ah. So you think they'd send you back there, but it's on the way?"

"Yep."

"Is it on the way to Dallas police headquarters?"

"I can see where you're going with that, Megan.

It ain't happening." This time his hand covered the entire bottom of his chin as he rubbed across his mouth.

The ranger had a tell. That particular one meant his mind wasn't made up. He was thinking about it. All she had to do was say the right thing that would convince him.

Wade Hamilton. That was her way to keep from being sidelined. "Just throwing this out there, but what if the message at your drop is time sensitive? I can stay safely in the vehicle."

"No."

"Look, Jack, we could argue about this for the next half hour until we reach Dallas, or we could be using that time to make a plan." *Nope, nope, nope. Mistake. I promised to stay in the car.* "I mean, just in case something goes wrong. But I'm sure nothing will."

He rubbed his chin again, considering it. Then he dipped it a couple of times. Not really a head nodding yes. Then it was.

"Just for the record, I was already considering it before you made the suggestion. So don't think you're manipulating me."

"It just makes sense. Especially if it's time sensitive."

"I already said yes. Mainly because you've been cleared of charges and I'm not sure why someone is insisting you be brought directly to the police.

Company B has already been placed in charge of the allegations because it's a Dallas city official."

"So why wouldn't they want me to come to your office ASAP?"

"Exactly." He switched the blinker on and exited I-35. "Until I understand why…you're safer with me."

"Is it that word-is-your-bond thing again?"

"Maybe. But it's more likely I want to finish a particular game of Battleship."

Chapter Twenty

Jack approached the drop like a normal driver. He slowed enough to catch the red light and be able to look. Nothing seemed out of place. It wouldn't. That was the point.

"That's a pretty wall. I love the building-sized bluebonnets. Can I help you look for something? If someone's watching, I could go pick it up."

"No. You're staying in the car. Give me your word, Megan."

"Sure."

"Stick out your hands and say the words."

"Do you believe I'd cross my fingers and not keep my promise?"

"Sure do. Stay here or next time you'll be cuffed to the steering wheel."

Palms up, she jabbed her hands toward him. He parked three streets away, gave her instructions in case he didn't return and left the keys. He didn't have any doubts at all that she would have followed him if he hadn't threatened her.

He walked around the block. At this time of day, this part of town, there wasn't anyone around. No windows looking onto the undeveloped street. That was part of the reason they'd come up with the spot.

He passed the painted wall with symbols from the state of Texas. The state flower, the American flag, a lucky horseshoe and a police seal. He did an about-face at the corner, doubling back to the downspout. He found the note behind the short hedge, wedged just above the bracket connecting it to the bottom turn.

The paper was damp from the morning dew, so he didn't open it, afraid that it might disintegrate before he could read the message. He ran around another block, approaching the lot where he'd left the car in from between two buildings.

Megan was sitting low in the driver's seat, engine running. He surprised her by tapping on the passenger window and was glad she didn't have a weapon. She'd shown a low-key, practical reaction to all their previous situations. This time she seemed nervous.

"You okay?" he asked as he got in.

Megan gripped the wheel like it was the last lifeline before hell, threw the car into gear and peeled out. Loose gravel flew, hitting the building behind her.

"Hey, either tap on the brakes or tell me what the hell's going on."

"Sorry." She slowed, heading back toward downtown Dallas. "Sorry. I was just so anxious. I mean, you had thirty seconds left before I was supposed to leave."

"And you were leaving?"

She turned her face toward him and away from the road so long it made him uncomfortable because she was driving. "Wasn't I supposed to?"

"Yeah," he agreed. "But I didn't think you'd do it. I thought you'd follow me. Since no one's on our tail, think we can pull over and take a look at this thing before it falls apart?"

"Yeah. Next vacant lot."

"Turn into this parking lot. We should be safe here." He didn't release the dashboard until she put his mother's car in Park.

She took a very deep breath and let it out slowly, shaking her shoulders. "That was exciting. So what does it say?"

Damn. That particular heart attack was with no real threat bearing down on them. "I'm driving from now on."

"Okay. Good. Yeah. Want to switch now?"

With the engine running, they met at the back of the car. Jack took her shoulders and pulled her to him. He kept her in his arms until he got her breathing slowed. Her pulse wasn't racing when she tipped her chin up to him.

"I swear I'm going to kiss you if you keep that look in your eyes," he said softly.

"Don't you dare. My heart just slowed down."

He wanted to stay there awhile longer with her wrapped in his arms, her cheek against his chest. He reluctantly let go and scanned the area. He'd been here before—the lot was normally full. Nothing out of the ordinary. Back in the car, Megan opened the note he'd left drying on the dashboard.

"It's a phone number. Why didn't he leave a message that said 'call me'?"

"Because that's not his number."

He dialed. No one answered. Jack was about to end the call when the voice-mail message clicked on and he heard his name.

"Jack. Thought this was the easiest way to explain what's going on," Wade said through the message. "I owed a favor to the people who located you at the border and got you to safety. The favor was keeping Megan Harper alive. Short story, I tracked down some answers—one is handcuffed inside my apartment and gave up the name Rushdan Reval. Yeah, weird name, right? Look the guy up. That's where I went for a look-see. I'll update this when facts change. Headed there now, twenty-one hundred Sunday."

The message ended and Jack was ready to yell at his partner. Hell, he might even shoot him if—and that was a big if—he was still alive.

"So do we wait?"

"*We* don't do anything. I need to find out who Wade's sniffing around." He knew what that particular message meant. And as jittery as Megan currently was…he didn't want her that way again.

"You should call the cavalry, then decide about the *we* part."

"Look, there's no way—"

"I didn't ask. You should call your buddies."

Explaining to Major Clements what had happened since last Friday afternoon couldn't be done quickly. Jack confirmed that no one else had heard from Wade in the past twenty-four hours. He summarized what they knew and informed the commander that the SUV guys had been able to trace them to an address that he hadn't visited in two years.

Then he was on hold while others were instructed to put a trace on Wade's phone and an initial research of Rushdan Reval was conducted.

Jack had no idea if he'd explained the situation accurately in the time frame needed to make a decision. It was out of his hands.

"You've been quiet. I'm not used to that."

"I can't change your mind about what you think is the best way to proceed."

He agreed but heard different words coming out of his mouth. "Do you have a better idea?"

Jack had worked with a partner for a long time—Wade for most of it. He might have been used to asking for opinions, but there was only one clear path for Megan today. She should be in protective custody. And as much as he wanted to provide it, to be the one who protected her, he owed Wade somebody in his corner who wouldn't give up.

Megan needed to be dropped with another ranger or someone at the DPS whom his commander trusted.

It didn't matter what she said. Right?

So why did he want her to convince him to stay by her side?

"Jack?" Major Clements came back on the line. "We think he was snooping around the Reval Wrecking Company properties on Rock Island."

"Dammit, that street is split in two by part of the river. Both parts of it are dead ends. Got any backup for me?"

"Already on their way. What's your location?"

"Dallas PD south of I-30. I'm five minutes from his location."

Surprised, Megan looked out the window. It

was obvious she'd missed all the signs while turning into the lot.

"I'll make a call and have someone ready for your witness and a team ready to accompany you. We need your eyes down there, but do not approach. They're bound to have surveillance."

"Yes, sir."

"And, Jack…don't do this on your own."

THEY WERE ALREADY at a police station. At least in the public parking lot of one. No uniform in sight, no black-and-whites or anything like that. If they'd had to drive somewhere, maybe—just maybe—she would have come up with a logical reason for her to stay with Jack.

Some way that she might have helped him find Wade. Instead, all they had to do was walk through the front door and she'd be handed off to strangers.

"You'll be safe," Jack said as if reading her mind.

"Let's get inside. Don't worry about me. You need to find your partner." She could take care of herself. She had done so before Texas Ranger Jack MacKinnon had come along… She could again. She wasn't angry or hurt. And if she kept reminding herself, she might actually believe it. This was a logical move. Not personal.

His eyes narrowed a bit as he reached for her

hand. "Do I have to ask if you're going to stay here, Megan?"

"You just did. Do I have to remind you that I'm not an idiot? Insisting that I tag along just makes me a liability. In fact, I'm very capable of taking myself through the front door, too."

Jack laced his fingers through hers. "I have to go inside anyway." He grinned, raising only one side of his mouth, giving her only half of the dimples she'd come to appreciate. He squeezed her hand. "You're right. You're very capable. Let's get this over with."

Dimples and reassurance. Two things she was going to miss about this man. Those things along with a bunch more—his good looks, humor, laughter, protection without being chauvinistic.

Oh, shoot, she was going to miss him. All of him. A lot.

She whipped around at a tap on her window.

"Excuse me?" a woman asked.

Jack rolled the window down a couple of inches. "Can we help you?"

"I was wondering if you knew where the door is. All I can find—"

Jack started the car, but it was too late.

The woman had a gun inside the car. "I wouldn't if I were you, Jack. I'm prepared to fire."

Jack killed the engine and raised his hands toward the car's roof. Megan did the same.

"Unlock the doors," the woman instructed.

Megan couldn't see much more than the woman's cheeks, overly large sunglasses and a scarf covering the woman's head. She should have been suspicious at the familiar sound of the woman's voice.

The door locks popped, and the woman got in behind Megan.

"Drive. It doesn't matter where," the woman said.

"You'll have to be a little more specific."

She dropped the scarf to her shoulders. "Oh, please, Jack, don't play the dumb ranger. I've been watching a friend of yours in that role all morning."

Megan turned at the voice. "Therese?"

"I am so glad you recognize me, honey." She tapped the seat. "I've only got a few minutes."

"Then you better talk quick. What the hell's going on?" Jack asked. "And how did you know we were here?"

"I've been waiting at the corner for an hour or so for you to show up. Wade thought this is where you might come after you got his message."

"Just who are you? And where the hell is Wade?"

"This is my friend Therese. She's the one who sent you to help me."

"Sorry about this. I thought it was necessary if

someone saw me get in the car." Therese put the gun in her lap. "I'll tell you everything you need to know, but I'd feel a lot more comfortable doing it away from here."

Jack put the car in gear and drove. Megan didn't watch. She twisted in her seat to get a better look at her friend. "Thank you. I might be dead if you hadn't sent Jack to me."

"Actually, I sent Wade. But he snooped a little too much and Rushdan's men caught up with him. I think that's when he called you, Jack, and why I video-conferenced. Wade eventually found his way here and got caught. I'll be lucky if they don't find that. You can circle around. I need to get back if this is going to work."

"What? Work for what?" Jack demanded, slamming on the brakes at a yellow light. "Explanations now."

"First we rescue your partner. The less you know, the better this should play out. After you drop me off, you can call Major Clements if you want and he can fill in whoever he's sending."

"No." Jack pulled off his mirrored shades and let them dangle from his fingertips. One arm perched on the steering wheel, one on the armrest. "No more working in the dark. Turn on a light bulb or I take you to the police."

Jack's weapon was now in his lap, at the fingertips of his right hand.

"Megan's probably told you that I left the academy. Truth is, I never did. I've been undercover, working my way up through the Reval organization. One of his fast moneymakers was selling properties that were in probate and torching them before the buyer discovered he didn't have the right to sell."

"Was Harry Knight in on it?"

"I don't have a lot of details, but with him out of the picture, they needed another scapegoat."

"Me?"

"When my supervisor wouldn't stop your takedown, I called Wade." She put the scarf back over her hair. "I wasn't going to let you die in order to save this operation."

"What are they looking for?" Jack asked, turning another corner.

"That's not only another story, it's classified. Today involves saving Wade. When I finally got to speak to him this morning, he told me about the message. If you barrel in there with SWAT and Rangers, he'll be killed and everything we've been working toward is done. But if you go in alone, you could make it look like he escaped. Take a look at this map."

Megan looked at a simple map with rights and lefts and a couple of codes.

"Memorize it. I can't let you keep it."

Trinity, fence, three rights, two lefts, nine, eight,

four, three, eight, six. She repeated the combination in her head. Nancy. Elephant. Fat. Tommy. Elephant. Sexy. Nancy's elephant's fat. Tommy's elephant's sexy.

"No! She's not going with me," Jack said, returning to the police-station parking lot.

Therese took the paper and opened the door. "I'm not sure how much longer Wade will be at that address. I wish I could do more."

Therese was gone before Jack could slide the gearshift to Park.

"Write down what she showed you."

"No. You heard her. There's not much time. You can't do this alone. We go together. Or you wait for SWAT. The team who breaks down doors first and who will most likely get your partner killed."

He put the car in gear. "Dammit."

Chapter Twenty-One

"The only way in just had to be coming up through a marshy riverbank. My feet are never going to be warm again." Megan laughed, but it was pretty much the truth.

"Time for silence," Jack whispered. "We're at the place where we should cut the fence."

They had ten minutes—tops—before the Rangers arrived with Dallas SWAT. He'd received the stand-down order from both units. Unfortunately, he knew that Megan was right. The men were the best, the top of their respective organizations, but Wade was a dead man if they waited.

If Therese was right and he wasn't dead already.

Jack had seen the numerous surveillance cameras along the street, at the corner of every building. Too heavy for the stores selling refurbished home parts. Old bathtubs, sinks and doors stored behind the locked gates weren't that valuable. Maybe the new, unfinished five-story building at the water's edge needed the upscale security. After all, they were about to break into it.

True to Therese's directions, there seemed to be a clear path between two of the junkyards once they were through the fence.

"This building seems out of place down here."

"Whoever Rushdan Reval is, he's building in anticipation of this turning into a Dallas river walk like the city of San Antonio. Now, no more questions or observations unless someone's on top of us holding a gun. Got it?"

"This isn't the first time I've done this. Well, maybe it is for, like, *this* specific—"

He shot her a look, and she knew what it meant. Wire cutters in hand, he clipped through the chain links quickly, efficiently and in silence. He'd verified he had the mag in his gun and the one in his pocket. Megan was unarmed.

They ran across the ground littered with building materials for the out-of-place office midrise. The door leading inside had been unlocked for the crew—all of which had conveniently left for the day. When you're about to murder someone, you tend not to want too many witnesses.

You better be here, Wade.

As they entered the building, Megan kept a hand on his back. She shifted it to his right or left to indicate which way the map had shown to go. They were a good team. Anticipating each other's steps and hesitations without encountering anyone.

It seemed like their luck was too good to hold, but they made it to the locked door where Wade had been kept a few hours earlier.

"Nancy's elephant's fat. Tommy's elephant's sexy," Megan chanted behind him. "I mean, nine, eight, f…four. Tommy. Elephant. Sexy."

It took him a minute to translate. "Nine, eight, four, two, eight, six?"

"Three, eight, six. I forgot there are two *t*'s. It's nine, eight, four, three, eight, six. Sorry. I'm just so nervous."

Jack punched in the code as she said it. The electronic lock indicator changed from red to green. He shifted the handle down to open the door, expecting something. Anything. He stopped Megan and verified the same code worked from the inside. Then they both stepped through and shut the door, plunging them into the pitch-black.

They both turned their cells on, using them as flashlights.

Lying on his stomach in the middle of an empty room about the size of a supply closet was Wade. Easily recognizable in a green camouflage hoodie that belonged to Jack. Kneeling, Jack felt for a pulse. "This isn't going to be easy. He's unconscious."

"Pick him up and let's go before someone—"

They both heard the footsteps in the hall and scrambled to get behind the door. Beeps from the electronic lock let them know they wouldn't be alone for long.

Jack pushed Megan behind him, protecting her as much as he could. The handle pushed down; the door cracked open. He was ready to hold them off until Dallas SWAT surrounded the building.

"Naw. This one's done and going upstairs to the boss. The dude in there still out?"

The door pushed open enough so someone could see Wade, then closed. The conversation was muted and stayed directly outside the door. Megan took out her cell phone and typed, then showed him the message.

Why do they have Alvie Balsawood from my office?

Jack shrugged. She typed again.

We can't leave him here.

He typed while the conversation involving the new prisoner grew louder. He shook his head and showed her the screen.

No choice.

But yeah, there was. If they had a cell signal…

They did. Dammit, he could coordinate an assault on the building. He'd give the code to the Rangers and have them pull Wade and Megan free. When SWAT hit the front, he could be up the stairs, where it seemed they were taking her coworker.

He could save him. Why hadn't Therese seemed concerned? Why had she scoffed that he was arriving and not given them details?

"Reval's ready. Bring him up," a louder voice said.

When all the voices faded, Megan brought her lips to his ear.

"What if he's the one who tried to frame me? It would make sense. Then again, what if he's not?"

His phone vibrated. They were out of time. The cavalry had arrived. He swiped the phone, placing it on speaker so they could both hear the plan.

"The major said I was to leave the yelling to him," Slate Thompson from his company said. "Don't think I'm going soft, but are you okay?"

"Great. Wade's the one in bad shape."

"Ambulance is around the corner. Do you have your location?"

"We entered from the rear of the building. It's about the size of a closet with an electric lock. Texting the keypad code."

"SWAT will be in position in three. We're going on four," said a voice from the background noise on Slate's end.

"Just warn everyone I'm here. We think the man responsible for framing Megan was taken to the second or third floor. I'll be securing him." Jack looked at his watch. "Three minutes. We'll be ready."

"Keep your heads down," Slate said. "Don't try to do anything heroic, Jack."

"You ARE GOING to be a hero, aren't you?" she asked.

"I should go after your friend."

Coworker.

Megan checked Wade for broken bones and to make certain he could breathe okay. "His ribs are probably broken. When I touch them, he's moaning even completely unconscious." Behind her, Jack discussed—softly and firmly—who would come to safely remove her from the building.

"Don't go all goo-goo-eyed over Slate. He knows he's handsome, so there's no reason to feed his ego," Jack teased. "You'll be fine here."

She wasn't arguing. With no weapon, she needed to stay put and be rescued. She'd have to think carefully about her word choices before she explained everything to her mom and dad. He'd want to know why she'd followed Jack into a hostile building without a weapon of her own.

Come to think about it, there had been plenty of pipe or even a board that she could have picked up. She hadn't thought about it until now. She took another look at Wade. The swelling around his left eye was huge. She spoke to him, but he was unresponsive.

Jack texted the code and then knelt by her to check on his partner. "He looks pretty bad."

"For the record, I'm glad I'm here to help you. Don't worry about us when you go up those stairs after Alvie."

"You're going to miss me?" He checked his watch.

"I've sort of gotten used to having you around." They stood and she hugged him. "Be careful."

"Kiss me for luck. One minute."

She raised her lips to his, and he captured them in a fierce, exciting rhythm. When they parted, he turned and put his hand on the door, waiting for the SWAT team to start all their fireworks.

The breach echoed through the building's steel. Jack was out the door without a second look. The door closed, and the light changed from green to red.

All she could do was wait. Muffled noises of shouting and running. Shots were fired. The door handle shook, but no one entered the code to release the lock. She stood close to the door, listening, trying to make out real words or sentences.

"Thanks."

"Oh my God. You're awake?"

"If I'd known you were so pretty, I would have made more of an effort to pick you up myself." Wade got the words out and coughed. A lot. Then did it some more as he pushed himself to a sitting position against the wall.

"You shouldn't try to talk. Or sit."

"That bad, huh?"

"Yes."

"Phone. You got one?" He coughed, grabbed his ribs and moaned.

"Really. You shouldn't try—"

"All a trap. Building's rigged to blow."

Chapter Twenty-Two

The second floor of the building was a shell like Jack had thought. Outside walls and windows were in place. That was about it. Heating and air-conditioning ducts were loose, some installed with many still lying on the concrete floor.

It only took a second to verify no one was waiting to ambush the men coming into the building. Everyone had to be on the third floor or maybe even higher. If he could give the major an estimate of men and guns, then rushing up those stairs after a potential murderer might be worth it.

Following someone into a building, even while on border patrol, had been limited and never without backup. While undercover, he'd mainly had backup from the gang.

Normally, he was much more prepared, forewarned about the number of men, their weapons, what to expect. He knew nothing about the man who owned the property or the man Megan had caught a glimpse of through the door-hinged gap. She seemed certain it was one of the men from her office.

Jack had no reason to doubt her. He trusted her. But the TDI employee showing up meant he was a victim like Megan or that the whole thing was his brilliant little scam.

Brilliant as in his father's words from the night before. Jack hadn't even had time to soak in the detailed information Therese gave them in the car. Approaching the third floor with caution, he slowed, not making noise.

The men downstairs were making enough noise to mask anything he created.

No one was around. These guys were either extremely confident or really understaffed. He didn't know which it was, but it was freaking him out a little.

Until…

Opening a door, Jack stepped into a very luxurious office. Lots of space. Lots of breakables. A view of the Dallas skyline that wasn't too shabby, but glance down and all you could see was junk.

One of the SUV guys was waiting for him in the center of the empty room.

"Great."

The one he'd rammed with his truck and pushed into the ditch. Bald, massive hands on hips, feet spread wide, smirk on his face. He looked like nothing could move him from his spot.

Jack didn't have a truck this time.

"I think somebody's been watching one too many movies," Jack said, pointing to the very large fish tank and a sheet of plastic over the carpet. "Let's hope your boss was protecting the rug from construction dust."

Why wasn't anyone else around? They must have run down another staircase in the front of the building. Shots fired, proving his theory that someone else had been there.

"So what's your name?" Jack asked.

The man three times his size cracked his knuckles and rolled his shoulders. Then Jack heard the crack of a spine as he tipped his head from side to side, getting ready to fight.

The witty insults normally came from Wade. "You look pretty tough. I could call you Sue, like the Johnny Cash song. But I'd need to know about your family history. Wanna share?" Occasionally Jack had his own. Like this one that had jumped into his head. The big guy didn't seem very impressed as he cracked his knuckles.

Should he wait for Sue Dude to ram him and knock him out with one punch? Each step the man took toward him meant he wasn't afraid Jack would fire. So Jack did the only thing he could... He fired.

He missed the fish by keeping his eyes on Sue Dude instead of looking away to where he aimed. He hit a very nice-looking painting or portrait. He put the bullet hole in the middle of the guy's head without trying.

"Well, would you look at that? I guess all those dates with the practice range have paid off."

Evidently, Sue Dude thought so, too. He dropped to his knees, raising his hands behind his head.

Cuffing this guy wasn't going to work. Jack didn't have any flex cuffs, and his metal bracelets wouldn't fit around the man's wrists—even if he'd had them. He pressed Sue Dude's chest into the plastic. Did he have time to wait on the SWAT team to secure the first two floors and begin this one?

Or the other option… Take Sue Dude with him.

That wasn't an option. Too many things could go wrong. What he needed was to find the TDI employee or get back to Megan. He couldn't leave this man to ambush SWAT or the Rangers.

"Dammit." Jack spun around the corner and aimed his weapon at a man with his hands in the air. "Who the hell are you?"

The cowering man stepped sideways, toward the fish tank. "Don't shoot. Don't shoot. I'm Alvie Balsawood. These men abducted me and tried to force me to perform illegal activities."

Sue Dude harrumphed into the plastic. What

wasn't he buying? That Balsawood had been abducted or forced? Jack's bet was that no one had forced him into a business relationship. Megan's coworker took another step.

"You're good where you are." Jack raised his hand and pointed.

Jack couldn't tell if Balsawood was purposefully getting to a position or if he was trying to shrink into the corner. Either way Jack didn't trust him, so he shifted his aim between the two men.

"Who are you?" Balsawood asked, his arms sinking to a more relaxed position.

"Lieutenant Jack MacKinnon, Texas Rangers."

"Texas Rangers?" Balsawood asked, dropping his hands to smack his thighs and moving forward. "Thank God. You're here to help."

"I gotta get up. This plastic smells funky."

"Stay back, Balsawood. Show me your hands." Jack kept both men in his view and wondered what was taking SWAT so damn long to get there. "Stay on your belly, Sue Dude."

"But aren't you here to protect me?" the weaker man whined, then looked at his watch.

"We can determine that as soon as—"

A blast from downstairs shook the building and rocked the floor under Jack's feet. Ceiling tiles fell, and building dust filled the air, making it hard to see.

"Finish him or lose everything," the cowering

man shouted from the corner. He shoved the tee-
tering fish tank and then ducked out the second
door where he'd come in.

Jack lost sight of Balsawood when Sue Dude
pushed himself from his knees, shoving a shoulder straight into Jack's gut. He kept his grip on his
gun, hitting the thick man in the side of the head.

No luck.

Sue Dude didn't flinch, just locked his arms
around Jack's midsection and tried to ram him
into the wall. Sue Dude lost his balance, tripping
over fish-tank decorations. But he kept his grip
as they crashed to the floor.

The wet plastic and flopping tropical beasties
kept either man from getting traction on the floor.
But when they used the furniture to pull them-
selves to their feet, Sue Dude evidently didn't like
fish or he liked them a helluva lot. He hopped
from one foot to the other, avoiding them as they
flopped.

If he'd had time to laugh, Jack would have.

Saved by a fish. No one would believe it.

THERE SEEMED TO be a lot of action for a building
that appeared to be basically vacant. Megan heard
yelling, running, weapons discharged. Wade had
passed out without giving her a lot of details. She
couldn't let anyone know, because her phone had
stopped working.

Maybe a jamming signal or phone service had just gotten more fickle inside the closet. She didn't know. Then she heard the beeps. The cavalry had finally made it to their door. She stepped away from the door, expecting to argue that she wasn't leaving until there was a stretcher for Wade.

Well...*that* didn't happen.

There was no running past the armed men who had come to finish off Wade. As the door opened, instead of facing Texas Rangers, Megan walked into a wall of burly chests. One of the men aimed a gun at her. The other said, "Move," pointing the gun barrel toward the hall.

Megan pulled the door shut behind her, engaging the automatic electronic lock.

"What about the ranger?" the one who had wanted to shoot her asked.

"He's dead," she said quickly and walked down the hall where she and Jack had entered, trying to get them away from Wade.

"And if he's not, he will be when this place comes down. Now hurry up."

Without entering the room and checking, they followed her until one yanked on her shirt and shoved her into another room. Then they pushed her through another door, which led to a staircase instead of a closet.

Still recovering from the moment of fear when she believed she'd be buried alive, her panic finally subsided enough for her to think. She didn't know where they were headed, but at least it seemed to be outside.

Hearing weapons fire was one thing, but the explosion a few moments ago had taken her breath away. Her hands shook so badly she laced them together, reminding her of each time Jack had held her hand.

Such a simple thing to do, but the pressure of his hand over hers had reassured her so many times. Just the thought of it now was having the same effect. She could escape, make a run for it through the junk they'd surveyed earlier.

The gunfire had died down. All Megan had to do was get to the front of the building. There were sure to be police officers that would help her.

Shoot, she could make it to the river and maybe swim her way out of this mess. The water behind the Wimberley house had been colder than what she'd waded through earlier today.

The man in charge looked at his phone. "Wait here while I see what's keeping the new guy."

"Wait here? We should be getting out of here fast. Did you see the men they sent after us? You'd think we were the Mafia or something," said the man who had wanted to shoot her. "I don't care how much the new guy is offering. We can't spend it if we're in jail."

The bigger, more in control man ignored the

man left with her and disappeared back the way they'd come.

"I don't blame you for being worried." Shoved first around a stack of wood and then to the ground, she sounded unnaturally calm as she reasoned with the young man holding the gun inches from her face. "You're right. You don't need me to get away without anyone seeing you were here."

She could take this guy. He seemed the weaker of the two, indecisive. Just wanting away from a bad situation. If she couldn't talk her way out... She shifted to her knees, ready to push herself up and ram her head into his bread basket.

"Who knows what we need?" said the one who'd taken her hostage as he rounded the stacked wood.

Megan immediately relaxed, but it was too late. He'd seen her ready to pounce and pulled zip ties from his jacket pocket.

"We ain't getting out through the front. The bomb thing the new guy set off stopped 'em from coming inside, but we're cut off back here." He pulled the plastic tight around her wrists. "You ain't going anywhere until we say so. Keep your mouth shut or I'll break your jaw so it can't move."

She winced as he pulled the plastic even tighter. She hated to give him the satisfaction of knowing he'd hurt her, but she couldn't help it. Her hands might be secure now, but she also knew they didn't have a real plan. She was insurance. But she could just as easily become a liability if she didn't cooperate. Her time to escape would come.

All she needed to do was get close to the water.

Before her excitement or fright—it was hard to tell which—could cloud her judgment, she locked both away. Whatever she felt, the young woman they'd killed and blown up in her home had received worse. Megan would find that woman's killers. They would be brought to justice.

How did Alvie fit into all this? Money, of course. That conclusion wasn't hard to jump to. She knew approximately how much he made, since everyone in the department didn't make much.

One thing was clear—he didn't have enough money to purchase the properties involved in this scheme on his own. If he had that much money, he wouldn't be working at the TDI. So maybe he was the brains and Reval was the money.

And for some reason, she was the scapegoat.

JACK YANKED A monitor cord free, putting both knees in Sue Dude's ribs. He jerked the big man's hands together, tying him like he would a calf for branding, with an extra permanent square knot to finish it off.

He stood by the window and dialed Clements to

tell him about Sue Dude. The system was either jammed or down from the explosion. Then he saw the boat. And they were moving Megan toward it.

Megan hadn't been taken in by her coworker. She'd assumed he was responsible as soon as she saw him, but she hadn't let that instinct condemn him. He ran after Balsawood, leaving Sue Dude on the wet floor, flopping like the fish he'd tried to avoid.

Jack had been taken by surprise by Balsawood and his bully. But even more by the explosion.

Why hadn't either of the men been surprised by the explosion like him? Dammit, they knew about the explosion. They'd planned it. How many of the SWAT team and Company B men had been taken down by it?

The stairwell was clear, but the doors to the second and first floors were blocked. He couldn't push the emergency-exit door open on either floor. So he kept going…after Balsawood, who would lead him to Megan.

Chapter Twenty-Three

Jack followed the stairs and the short dark tunnel, where he shoved the door open to brilliant sunshine. No one fired at him, but he ducked his head before venturing through. The door shut with an electronic lock, making it impossible to reenter.

A cleverly hidden escape route. The door was disguised on the lot next to the new building by a stack of secondhand doors.

He tried the phone again while he ran between old salvaged parts from homes. He knocked into a row, sending doors tumbling backward like dominoes into a shed wall.

There was barely a path in front of him, but he recognized where he'd seen Megan from the river-view window of Reval's office.

"Megan!" he shouted.

"They have a boat," she yelled.

Her shout was followed by a sound that he recognized…the thud of a fist on bone. The bastard had hit her.

Whoever had hit her would… He tightened his knuckles into a fist. They'd feel at least one hard punch from him. At least one.

The anger building inside him fired up his legs. He ran through the strips of old flooring, kicking an occasional piece of porcelain. His boots crunched the broken glass from windowpanes as he swatted six-foot-tall grass and reeds.

Dammit. How had they taken her hostage?

The odds that Wade was still alive got worse. Those men had probably gone to that closet to kill him— Tying up loose ends. Now they had a hostage… Megan.

He had to finish this and reach her before they made it to the boat.

Jack rounded a corner into an arm extended with a .45. Training took control as he stopped thinking until the threatening weapon was on the ground and he was kicking it under a pile of sinks.

Using all his might, he rammed a sore shoulder into the man's gut—kid, really—and they tumbled onto a pile of bathroom hardware. The young man landed a hard fist in Jack's side. Already bruised from Sue Dude's punches, Jack gritted his teeth against the pain.

"You the one who hit my girl?"

"No. No. No. That wasn't me. Let me go, man.

I don't know nothin'." The kid threw a useless punch, connecting with air.

"Where is he taking her?"

Jack threw his own fist to crack the kid's jaw, then clamped his mouth shut to stop the groan of pain he wanted to release. His knuckles and lots of other body parts were already raw from his earlier fight.

They rolled in a deadlock, equally matched because Jack was tired.

The kid groaned after a flip to his back when Jack landed a knee close to his groin. Then they reversed and broke apart as Jack narrowly avoided a furious foot slamming onto his chest.

Back on his feet, he locked his arm behind the kid's head but couldn't finish the defensive move without snapping his neck. He needed a minute to catch his breath and decide what to do.

There should have been an entire SWAT team through the building by now. "Where the hell is everybody?" Since they weren't around, he'd have to release this guy in order to follow Megan.

An explosion ten times larger than the first shook the ground like an earthquake. Debris filled the air, turning it to a chalky white cloud. The unfinished building on the next lot collapsed, upper floors to lower.

Stunned, Jack let the kid he'd been fighting

run, escaping the wreckage that was still settling on the ground.

"Megan? Megan!"

"OH MY GOD!" Megan jerked free of the man holding her shoulder. The explosion wasn't a surprise to her captor. He'd covered his head, and that was about it.

Jack is not inside. Jack is not inside. Please be okay.

"What have you done? All those men are... Please let me go. I can help them."

"Pipe down. You should worry about helping your own self."

Near the riverbank she'd navigated with Jack only an hour ago, Alvie Balsawood and Therese stepped out from behind old building materials. Therese averted her eyes, not making contact.

"We're getting in that boat, getting across this river to the park, stealing a car, then driving away from here." Balsawood tugged her close to him. "You know what's going to happen. We've only got a few minutes."

"You're not in charge," Therese said. "But we have the same objective, so I'll work with you. For now."

Alvie pointed a gun at her abductor. "Send her through the fence or I'll shoot you both. I don't want to, but I will." He ended with a weird, crazy laugh that shook his round body.

Gooseflesh popped out across Megan's arms. She didn't believe him. He sounded like he *did* want her dead.

The man who had abducted her shrugged. "All I want is to get away from a bad situation, man."

He didn't act like he cared. In fact, he put away his gun and held the wire open so Megan could get through it.

A little farther along the bank was the boat that Alvie had shouted about.

"Pick this thing up so we can get onto the river," Alvie instructed them all. He stood apart from them, waving the gun like a fan.

Therese ignored her. Even as they struggled to carry the small rowboat across mushy sand and silt. What she thought was the Trinity River was actually just stagnant water caught in an overflow area. Once they made it across the forty yards to the main water, then what? Did he plan to take her with him? Would Therese keep him from killing her?

What was her plan? Get across the river and run? No. She couldn't trust him.

Alvie was crazy. She would capsize that rowboat. She didn't envy another dunk in the cold November water, but she would not be this man's hostage. This bastard had blown up her house and had taken down that ten-story building. He wouldn't do anything else to her.

"I could carry this boat better if you untied my hands," Megan said, standing from trying to free her shoe in mud.

"Not a chance," Alvie said. "It's too much fun."

"Why are you doing this? You…you killed all those police officers."

"Maybe, but no one will ever prove it. All the evidence points to you. I'm too smart for them to catch. It's just not going to happen."

They finally made it to the Trinity. The man who was following Alvie's orders held the boat at the water's edge while Therese and the crazy man got inside.

"You, too, Megan."

She hesitated.

"Run and I'll have him shoot you. Whatever. It no longer matters to me. Let's go."

The man took out his gun. Megan was getting really tired of having one pointed at her. She climbed inside the smallish rowboat and prepared herself for the necessary. The oars were bungeed to the inside. Therese and Alvie removed them and stuck them in the water while the man climbed in. The current took them swiftly away from shore.

The farther they got, the harder it would be for

her to get back with her hands still secured by the zip ties. So she acted fast. It was too simple.

One second they were inside the rowboat… The next, they were all in the murky Trinity.

Chapter Twenty-Four

Jack watched the rocking of the small boat. Then it capsized. He pushed through the cut fence, hearing his shirt rip, feeling the flesh scratch beneath. Not caring about either. He calculated the driest route to the Trinity, stopped on the bank and tugged off his boots and dropped his gun and cell.

Four heads bobbed near the flipped rowboat. Two people immediately started swimming for the far side—away from the police and building rubble. Two were trying to grab hold of the hull. One's hands were clasped together.

Megan.

Jack ran as far along the riverbank as he could before diving into the water. He caught up to find Balsawood climbing on top of Megan. She was completely underwater. Jack caught a fistful of

Balsawood's shirt and punched him in the nose as best he could while floating in water.

Megan sputtered and sucked in air, flailing her wrists through the air until her eyes connected with Jack.

"Relax and let me tow you to shore."

"He'll…he'll get away."

"Forget it, Megan! I'm getting us to shore."

She nodded. He put his arm under hers, resting across her chest, and swam. It wasn't far, but during the same amount of time, the rowboat completely went under.

Megan was on her knees in the dirt, spitting up river water. Jack kept banging on her back, forcing more coughing to get up water.

"Oh, God, where did he go? Did he go under? He can't get away."

Jack didn't care. Balsawood was someone else's problem now. "Did you think that stunt through at all?"

She turned in circles, searching the riverbank. "He's crazy. If you had looked into his eyes and seen what I did… You would have tipped the boat to get away, too." Her eyes stopped searching the riverbank and landed on Jack's face.

He grabbed the plastic tying her wrists together, emphasizing the tied portion that wouldn't let her move her arms. "I might have thought twice before capsizing a boat when I couldn't swim."

"Are you…? You are! You're actually mad at me." She looked astonished but smiled and laughed.

"Why would you think— Okay, I admit it." He hugged her body to his chest, glad she was alive. "I almost lost you."

Megan placed her hands on either side of his chin, used her thumb to draw circles over the dimple she teased him about, then pulled his face to hers. "I missed you, too."

They had to get back to the building, find out if anyone had gotten Wade out. He held her close as they walked back to his boots. So why couldn't he bring himself to let Megan go?

"Why me, Jack?" she whispered. "I barely know Alvie Balsawood. I live a simple life. No family. I keep my head down and do my job. I'm boring."

She kept turning in circles, obviously looking for her coworker, who had come to shore farther downstream.

"Maybe that's exactly what made you the perfect fall guy—girl. I mean, there's no one around to dispute or question your involvement."

"Did you see where Alvie went?"

How she switched from sexy-as-hell woman to vulnerable victim to practical law officer, he hadn't a clue. But it worked on her. And he liked it.

"Downstream. If I were him, I'd be trying to get

to the street through that junkyard." He dumped the sand from his boots and yanked them back onto his feet.

"I think the sign said it was more like reusable home supply parts. All these lots are."

"Whatever it is, there are plenty of places to hide. And no one but us is looking for him." He swiped his wet hair back away from his eyes.

The sirens were deafening. The flashing lights were fragmented through the white cloud, thick with smoke and small particles that hovered where the building had been. He wondered…

"It feels like a war zone out there." Megan grabbed his hand first for once. "Do you think Wade was still—"

"Can't go there. None of the first responders will be allowed in the building until the bomb squad verifies there aren't any other explosives. They won't be on the river side of things for a while."

"Can we call?"

"Nothing." He showed her the screen with no connection.

"I hate that he's getting away with this. Alvie admitted to me that he set those bombs and fires, killing all those people." She tugged on his hand to get him moving. "Let's go. We can't let him get away."

"Oh, no. You aren't going anywhere."

"If we argue we're just going to be wasting time. I'm in this up to my eyeballs, so let's go." She dropped his hand and took off running.

She was wrong, but he had no way—or right—to hold her back. He caught up with her, slowing her down while they entered the property where part of the fence had fallen.

"Stay smart. Quiet. And let me take him down."

"I haven't seen you carrying a knife. Right?" She lifted her hands, still locked by flex cuffs at the wrists.

He shook his head. "Maybe the office has scissors."

"Good idea." She darted past him.

He pulled her back. He might not be able to keep her from being with him, but he sure as hell could force her to stay behind him. And his weapon.

"We don't know if he came in here or not. Let's get to the office and trust that he'll be caught. We're at risk of being shot by both sides."

"You think the cops will shoot at us? Or your friendly Rangers? Do you think they were in the building?" she asked.

The jolt of agony that his company could be gone blasted through his entire body. "I honestly don't know. They'll be clearing every building around here. If you see them, don't try to explain. Just drop and wait."

A bullet pinged off the tin lean-to they were under. That wasn't the cops. Jack turned and discharged his weapon to keep the shooter from firing again.

"I see the office." He pointed, then grabbed her shoulder with his free hand, forcing her to look at him. "I'll lay down cover and you run. We go through the office. Once on the street, put your hands up. They're going to assume we're part of whoever brought down the building."

His hand dropped, letting her go. He stepped out, took a couple of shots, and she took off. He saw her weaving in and out of junk, not letting the gunfire slow her down.

Too late he realized that there was movement just ahead of Megan, heading for the office. He ran faster to catch up, but the door opened and she disappeared inside. He followed, entering the office area more cautiously.

The lights were off. He stayed low. Most of the sounds he heard were from outside. Rescue workers. Someone shouted, "All clear." But the low bumps and grunts he heard led him to the front counter.

The sound of frustrated efforts of trying to cut through plastic sent relief through his soul. "Megan," he whispered. "Don't swing the scissors." He rounded the counter and joined her on the floor.

"Thank goodness. Can you…?" She placed the scissors in his right hand as he switched his gun to the left. Quickly, they freed her of the restraints.

"He didn't go through the door. It's still bolted at the top."

"You leave. Remember what I told you about surrendering yourself."

"I like my chances better next to you, Ranger." She put her hand on his shoulder.

Relief again. He didn't have to worry about her if she was with him. They could pin Balsawood down together. "Did you try the landline?"

She picked up the phone. No dial tone. Either the feds—who would have joined the scene after the bombs—or the local PD had shut everything down. Standard operating procedure.

"Keep the scissors."

"Definitely.

They moved through the maze of bins with old doorknobs and mailboxes. Anything and everything that could be salvaged from an old house was there. He moved, and Megan moved, anticipating his direction. Teamwork.

Then Balsawood darted from a smaller room, running in the dim light back the direction where they'd entered the office.

"You don't have to do this, Balsawood. We can work things out. No one will ever know you're a witness. They have programs for that," Jack shouted.

"It's too late. I'm not going to jail. I'm sorry, but running is my only chance."

"Don't be crazy, Alvie. That guy who owns all this property… What's his name? Oh, Rushdan… Rushdan Reval, he has to be behind this. All you have to do is tell the police what happened. You can make a deal," she pleaded.

Her coworker ran down the next aisle. "I'm not going to jail. Stay back. Stay back or I'll shoot!" Full of panic, his voice shook like a soprano's. It was so different from that of the man at the river. "I'm getting out of here."

"There isn't anywhere to run," Megan tried.

Alvie tripped and fell from her view, screaming in agony. She couldn't see what had happened, but it sounded like he was dying. Gun or no gun, she ran toward the cry of pain. She rounded the corner, Jack tugging at her to slow down. Alvie had fallen onto an antique window. The frame still held part of the glass, and a sharp spear of it had pierced his thigh back to front.

"Let me have your shirt," she said as soon as Jack got to her.

He verified Alvie was free of weapons, then untucked his shirt from his belt, unbuttoned the top and pulled it inside out over his head. It was wet from the river, but that didn't matter.

Alvie had tried to frame her and have her murdered, but she didn't want him to die. So she wrapped Jack's shirt around the edge of the glass, trying to stop the blood. Her coworker pleaded and cried the entire time.

"We can't call for help with everything jammed. I'll stay here while you go," she told Jack. "I'll be fine."

"I think that's what we agreed the last time."

"I've heard more first responders. I'm sure they've rounded everyone up. Go. I promise not to be dragged away again."

She was almost surprised when he actually left. The main door opened—she heard the bell—and the noise from the chaos at the bomb site grew.

"Why would someone blow up a building and hurt so many people?"

"To get away, idiot. I can't believe they said you were more qualified than me." Alvie shifted, screamed and settled back to the floor. "Those stupid policy setters at TDI who thought hiring ex-cops was a better idea than someone with my higher thought process."

"You set those bombs?"

"Of course I did, but you'll never prove it. I covered my tracks. All the fires, the paperwork… none of it can be traced back to me. You'll never find my money."

"I know about the insurance fraud. We'll eventually find everything."

She wanted out of there. Wanted to lift her hands from keeping pressure on the wound and leave. But she wouldn't. She was a better person than this lowlife.

"The last bit was so easy. I paid the men he sent to bring me here. Not much. Just a little more." He cried. "If I got rid of him first, then he couldn't get rid of me."

"Anyone in here?" a voice shouted from the direction of the door.

"Over here," she answered.

Megan moved back so the rescue workers could work. She was still in shock at what a normal-seeming guy like Alvie Balsawood was capable of doing when Jack called out and found her. He tugged her to her feet and wrapped his arms tight. His strength seeped through his muscles into her. She didn't cry. Even when she wanted to give in to tears for all the people caught in the anger from one man's jealousy.

"He did it. Everything. He bragged about all the explosions and fires. I thought he wanted money, but I think it was about my job. He's... I think he's just crazy." She lifted her hands, stained with his blood. "I really need this off me. Now. Get it off. Where's a restroom?" She jerked free from his hold and rubbed her hands up and down her thighs.

"Megan. Megan, look at me." Jack shook her shoulders a little and forced her to keep eye contact with him. "Babe, you're in shock. We're going outside and we'll get you cleaned up. I promise."

"Okay."

She let him guide her through the fire trucks, the ambulances, the bomb-squad guys removing their gear and the too-many-to-count police officers.

"Hey, Slate. Give me a hand."

A man wearing a Texas Ranger badge ran up to them, slapping Jack on his shoulder. "I told those guys you were too smart to go down with a building."

"Megan's in shock, probably needs to be checked out—"

"I'm fine," her voice said in one of those moments when a person was doing things, but totally unsure how. She stood straight, patted Jack's hands and kept walking toward an ambulance. "But I am seriously wet. Think they have a blanket?"

Chapter Twenty-Five

As often as Jack had looked at Therese, she'd never made eye contact. Not even when they wheeled Wade past everyone on a stretcher. Now the woman behind Jack's rescue at the border was in handcuffs along with the men who had been fighting. They were all on their knees, shoulder to shoulder at the edge of the street.

Jack had been watching them until his company commander ordered him to have his injuries looked at by the EMTs. He finally joined Megan at the edge of the commotion.

"Not only am I homeless, I'm also phoneless." Megan set her cell on the hood of the police car, then twisted her T-shirt, wringing water from the bottom. "I have no way to contact any person I know."

"But you still have your health." Jack picked up the blanket and hung it around her shoulders.

She sneezed. "I'm not too sure about that anymore."

"So I was thinking…" Jack rubbed his chin, contemplating. "I sort of need a date for homecoming Friday and Saturday. Want to come and… um…sleep with me again?"

The meaning wasn't lost on Megan. She winked and smiled. "You're ready for me to sink your battleships?"

The first responders standing near enough to overhear gave them a weird look. They weren't a part of the inside joke.

"You can try." He leaned in closer. "But we both know who was winning."

"In all honesty, I'm not sure I'm the appropriate date for your homecoming. I was raised where football is what Americans call soccer. My senior year in Texas, I totally didn't get what football fever was all about."

"Then that's a date. You need someone to explain everything and treat you right."

"Of course, this is all contingent on our names being cleared—by someone other than your father. And giving whatever statement is needed to put that terrible creep—" meaning Balsawood "—in jail forever."

"I still think we can make it home by Thursday."

Home? She didn't have a home any longer. Straightening that out would be a nightmare.

"I can see where your mind went. The wheels are spinning about how you're going to get everything done and where to start."

"How do you do that?" No one had been able to read her so well before.

"There will be enough time next week to start the slow bureaucratic insurance and paperwork. Right now I think you need a break. Come with me."

He put his hand firmly on the small of her back and guided her to a man placing a white hat on his balding head. "Major Clements, this is Megan Harper. She saved Wade's life."

"Nicely done, Miss Harper. I must apologize that you were put in that position." He took her hand, clasping it between both of his. "Thank you for your courage this weekend and for the help in bringing these men to justice."

"I think it was a team effort, and I was glad to be a part of it. Especially since they protected me so well." Lost house and all. She was alive, and she'd met Jack. And he was worth every on-the-run, nerve-racking minute.

"Fair warning, sir. I don't consider that Megan was either a prisoner or a witness for the past four days. I'll be referring to our encounter as a favor for a fellow ranger. It might complicate things, but it's the truth." Jack took her hand in his, leaving no doubt in his commander's mind.

"I don't believe it complicates matters too much, Jack. Just tell the truth."

She waited for the commander of Company B to leave before she gave Jack a stinky look. "Why did you do that?"

"Tell the truth?"

"You could have given me a heads-up you were going to tell the world about us. Especially since there isn't an us."

"Oh, come on. I didn't— No, forget that. I very much intended for everyone around here to know you're my girl. Give me this weekend. See if we can have some fun instead of wading through freezing rivers. Deal?"

"Your girl?" She kept walking, not staying mad at him if she ever had been. Irritated maybe, but not angry. "Okay, but there better be food in the refrigerator." She turned to him and poked him in the chest. "Real food, Jack. Something that goes in the microwave and comes out ready to eat."

He caught her hand, entwining his fingers through hers. "I'll be sure to stop by the frozen-pizza section."

"Damn straight."

Chapter Twenty-Six

Yesterday, Jack had experienced one of the longest days in his career as a law officer. Interview after interview. Grand-jury testimony next week. Closed depositions. Waiting was the only break, and that was more painful than testifying.

But his part was over for the weekend. They'd flown back to Austin and rented a car for the rest of his vacation in Liberty Hill. Driving by what was left of Megan's house depressed her. Thank God he'd already convinced her to stay with him for homecoming.

Megan was officially on leave until she was cleared for work again. She kept insisting she was fine, but he was glad her department realized she needed time to recover.

Today had been full of last-minute homecoming details, an alumni dinner and a private chat with his dad. In fact, the last bit had been Jack leaning into the passenger window of his dad's car. He'd been floored when his dad agreed with him and finally accepted that Jack was happy as a Texas Ranger.

Maybe he'd run for office after he retired, but for now…this was what he wanted. He came inside a dark house, locking the door after him and believing that Megan had already gone to bed. A couple of steps in, she lit candles.

"How's Wade? You called him at dinner, right?" she asked.

"The swelling's gone. No permanent damage. I don't know how they're sure of that. I mean, maybe he already had brain damage, considering how erratic his behavior was prior to this thing."

"How can we be mad at him? He's the reason we're here, together. And Therese, of course."

"I'll be filling out paperwork because of him for a month. But let's not talk about my partner or your friend who's undercover for who knows who."

Wade was officially still his partner this week. Jack had spoken to him long enough to confirm he'd been released from the hospital that afternoon. As Megan turned around from the kitchen table, any thought about his partner flew out the window.

She untied the belt around the robe before she sat on the couch. She curled her legs under her but left the robe open, teasing him with what was underneath.

"Uh… I see you've made yourself at home."

Covered in as many pieces of clothing as she'd worn when he'd carried her to bed last weekend, Megan had a brand-new Battleship game set up for them to play.

"You ready to finish our game? If I remember correctly, you were down to your jeans."

Off came his boots, socks and shirt. He grabbed a couple of beers and planned his board from the other end of the couch.

The matches went back and forth, and the room got warmer and warmer as they shed one piece of clothing at a time. Hotter still when he called out what should be the last letter and number. "B nine."

"Oh. Darn." She pouted without conviction. She stood and the robe dropped off each shoulder, leaving her beautifully naked, taking his breath away. "You sank my battleship."

MEGAN ALREADY KNEW that Texans took their football seriously. But she'd never witnessed high-school football champions or the rally to create more.

Everywhere they walked through town, people came up and shook Jack's hand. They'd use his nickname, he'd roll his eyes, but the smile on his handsome face never wavered. Then, without fail—woman or man, old or young—each would ask who she was and if they were an item. It was cute, if not exhausting.

And she secretly loved every minute.

Along with past homecoming kings and queens, Jack was introduced from the sidelines as the quarterback and captain who had last won the state championship. He held Megan's hand in his and waved to the crowd with the other.

"Tell me the truth. Did you know the school was going to retire your jersey?" Megan asked. "You seemed genuinely surprised."

"They've only retired two jersey numbers before. No one dropped a hint." He set the framed jersey against the fence, picked her up and twirled her around. The band was still coming off the field, and several of the drummers made kissy noises.

"There is only one response to juveniles. Lead by example." Megan kissed Jack with a lot of self-restraint, keeping it PG-13. When she was done, he let her feet touch the ground again to a round of high-school applause.

They sat in the stands, and everyone in the town of Liberty Hill and some from Leander—including Carl Ray and Nelva—stopped by to say hello and congratulations. The team won the football game and would be heading for the playoffs the following week.

Football game over, the nachos and popcorn eaten and with all but a few of the crowd returning to their homes, Jack walked her to the car. They strolled past the storefront windows decorated with "Beat the Bobcats" on the way back to the rental parked behind the police department.

"So what now? Anything else happening tonight? Is there a dance or another— What was that stunt you broke up called last night?"

"Cow tipping after the bonfire."

"Oh, right. I loved the bonfire, by the way. It was the first time in a week I haven't been cold."

"You know we have to be up early to organize the parade. And we've been going nonstop all day. I'm feeling like an old man. Aren't you ready for bed?"

"I'm willing to be sleep deprived for a repeat of last night. What about you?"

"Tonight and every weekend I can manage."

Jack kissed her, warming her like the bonfire the night before.

"What are you going to do on your forced vacation?"

"Find a place to live. Figure out how to replace everything."

"You know you can stay at my place. I mean, it's only a forty-five-minute commute. It's not like we'd be living together or anything. You know I've got the job and apartment in Dallas during the week. You can even pay rent if it makes you feel better, but the house doesn't cost me anything, so you don't have to. My grandmother left it to me."

Perfect timing. He pulled into the driveway and cut the lights. The house looked warm and welcoming with its golden porch light and rocker behind the rail. The inside could use a little more up-to-date homeyness, and the backyard needed a puppy.

She was sure Jack would be great with another dog, and some modern curtains, a few plants and a freezer full of frozen ready-to-prepare food.

"What do you think? You ready to give whatever chemistry this is between us a try?" Jack smiled, showing off his dimples. "If you're not sure…" He winked. "I could attempt to convince you."

Yes. The word was on the tip of her tongue. She was ready to say yes in a heartbeat.

But having him convince her sounded like a lot more fun.

* * * * *

Look for the next book in USA TODAY
bestselling author Angi Morgan's
TEXAS BROTHERS OF COMPANY B
miniseries, RANGER DEFENDER,
available next month.

And don't miss the titles in her
previous miniseries
TEXAS RANGERS: ELITE TROOP

BULLETPROOF BADGE
SHOTGUN JUSTICE
GUNSLINGER
HARD CORE LAW

Available now from Harlequin Intrigue!

Get 2 Free Books,
Plus 2 Free Gifts —

just for trying the
Reader Service!

Get 2 Free Books,
Plus 2 Free Gifts –

just for
trying the
**Reader
Service!**

STRS17R2